BEAR
HIS MARK

Wylde Den, Book One

TALINA PERKINS

For information contact; address www.talinaperkins.com

Book and Cover design by Bookin' It Designs

ISBN-13: 978-1545370285
ISBN-10: 1545370281

First Edition: May 2017

10 9 8 7 6 5 4 3 2 1

Raves for Talina Perkins

Bear His Mark

"Talina Perkins brings readers drama, romance, suspense and action in this paranormal romance. This tale is a spicy and fun read. The story is well-plotted out, superb, and entertaining." -*Top Pick, Night Owl Reviews*

"I have a huge crush on the Wylde Men! I loved this story and was immediately drawn in. I would recommend this to any and all of my reader friends." –*Judy McNeil, Reader Review, 5 Stars*

Bear His Bond

"Werebear Everett Wylde days as a player are numbered. His bear wants its mate, the wildlife veterinarian Pepper Cambridge. They make a spicy combination. Talina Perkins has blazed the heat level up a few notches in this story. She finds creative ways for the use of scarves and dessert. Readers will need a fan or an iced cold drink after reading it."- *Top Pick, Night Owl Reviews*

"This story unfolds beautifully with an emphasis on adventure, intrigue, hot sex and the couple realizing they had a true bond that shouldn't be ignored. I recommend this book to anyone who loves paranormal romance and adventure." - *Diane Page, Reader Review, 5 Stars*

Bear Their Secret

"Cherry desperately wants a family but is afraid to trust again. Thankfully she's got not one but TWO sexy alpha shifters willing to change her mind. What a lucky girl! I love Talina Perkins romances. She understands the power of family with great suspense and awesome love scenes. Next please!"-*Author Jennifer Hilt, 5 Stars*

"Another great part to the Wylde brother Den...I loved this one - the chemistry and bond between Cherry, Lorne and Kohl was great...I absolutely love this series and can't wait to read more by Ms. Perkins." -*Jenny H., Reader Review, 5 Stars*

Snowbound with Her Christmas Bear

"Talina Perkins has a way of drawing you into the story from the first scene... Once she has you hooked, she keeps you involved by providing alpha males, three dimensional characters, a mystery and the growth of the relationship between Sabine and Rone. I really enjoyed Ms. Perkins' writing and this story. I would highly recommend it." - *PamD, Reader Review 5 Stars*

CHAPTER ONE

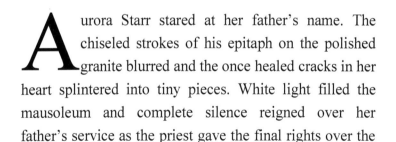

Aurora Starr stared at her father's name. The chiseled strokes of his epitaph on the polished granite blurred and the once healed cracks in her heart splintered into tiny pieces. White light filled the mausoleum and complete silence reigned over her father's service as the priest gave the final rights over the empty crypt.

Empty because her father refused to do anything the easy way in life, so why should he in death?

Thunder rumbled in the distance as if the heavens felt her pain. Tears welled along the rims of her eyes to wet her lashes, but she willed them away. Tiny nails pierced the tender flesh of her palms. Slowly, cautiously, she slid her eyes closed and focused on the pain. That she could handle.

She sniffled and dug into every last ounce of strength in her body, straightened her back as the final prayer for her father drew to an end. For the past hour dozens of eyes had been glued to her every move. Only now did she feel a small reprieve as everyone bowed their heads.

Tears never helped anyone. We can learn a lot from the diamonds we pull from the earth. Cold and hard. Take a lesson and life will be easier.

That was her father all right. Cold-hearted and razor sharp.

But not always. Tears fell for that father. The one that loved the outdoors and loved life. Not the jaded and torn man he became.

Her father's words ran chills up the length of her spine as though he stood over her shoulder, ready with one quip or another the second she showed signs of actually feeling something. They'd grown apart over the last couple of years. His bitterness toward her working for the other kind bled into her life until she had no choice but to sever ties. She'd asked for his understanding yet all she got in return was a note on corporate stationary each

Christmas with a few crisp Benjamins tucked inside. As if his money would solve everything between them. But still, with him gone now, nothing would be the same.

As long as she could remember he always wielded a high hand over her life. He'd ruined it once five years ago on the cusp of her mother's gruesome death. Maybe if she would have played the passive, obedient daughter they could have been happier. It all seemed moot now anyway.

"Will you be all right, darling? Why don't you come home with us and stay a while? I'll make up the spare bedroom." Her aunt eyed the two trench coats flanking her, their grim faces half hidden behind black tinted glasses despite there not actually being any sunshine to speak of. The raised collars didn't do much to conceal the earpieces and holsters.

She narrowed her eyes at them and mentally tacked on another thing to her massive to-do list.

"I know you love spending the spring there. It'll help take your mind off of everything." A soft, weathered hand to her arm brought her head around and the second Father Gracing slid his Bible closed, her unassuming aunt pulled her into a heartwarming bear hug. All five-foot, one hundred pounds worth of little old lady made everything better with her Aunt Bea worthy apple pies and kind soul. Don't forget the chicken soup. A nice big bowl of that would be ten times better than what she had to do now.

Beyond the doors, limos lined the gravel road that led to the private Starr mausoleum. Another reminder of her arranged fate as the assessor of her father's company.

Three generations of her family rested here. Uncles, aunts, her mother, and now her father. If only in spirit. All had a hand in building Starr Gem Global, the diamond empire that would be hers within a week whether she wanted it or not. From diamond princess to ice queen. Or, as her father would say, from the gutter with the animals to the leaders of the modern world.

Jaded and bitter didn't begin to describe her father.

Butterflies brushed against the soft interior of her stomach. Her breath quickened.

Out of the corner of her eye, she caught a tall, stocky man who towered over several grievers, his eyes glued on her. News crews waited along the gate, their cameras at the ready.

It all came at her at once. He was gone. She'd take anything over the silence eating at her insides.

She scanned over the room. Not one person beyond her aunt and uncle looked familiar, but everyone knew her. Maybe she wasn't cut out for this.

With a gentle squeeze, Aurora pulled back from her aunt and looked down on the icy blue eyes of the woman that helped raise her after the passing of her mother. How long before she'd leave her too?

"I... I have to go. I'm sorry. I can't right now." No matter how tempting hiding out from the ugly world appealed to her, she had a promise to keep before... before whatever happened after losing her father and gaining an empire in the expanse of a week.

"Are you sure, darling? Your father would be so disappointed."

Aurora dragged out a smile and slipped it on for her aunt's sake. "I have to do something for him." And herself, depending on how you looked at it. Either way, it would take her away from here if only for a little bit. "You know how Father is—was—with a promise." She swallowed hard. The time away would help clear her head.

"Child, you're too hard on yourself. Is it something I can help with?" The understanding and kind heart her father lacked, her aunt made up for in spades.

Something warm and wet hit her hand where her aunt clasped her close. Oh! One more teary-eyed plea and she'd have no more willpower to say no or leave her aunt to grieve the passing of her brother alone.

Rumbling split the skies once again, this time promising to make good on its threat.

"I won't be gone long. A day or two, tops. Promise."

"Things are about to change, Aurora. You have to be ready."

Her aunt's eyebrows shot up and her eyes turned a shade of blue that denoted determination. All the Starr women had it. Her father called it the Starr-pointed look.

Aurora crossed her heart and tucked away the invisible key in her pocket like they used to do when she was a little girl. That seemed to do the trick. Her aunt graced her with a smile and patted her hand.

"Go, child. I'll cover for you."

Bless her sweet heart.

A familiar, deep, level voice carried over the crowd. Angling her body toward the parked cars, Aurora took a step back one last time. Shit. Her uncle was headed their way, most likely to take her aunt home and with him came another set of stiff, by-the-book trench coats.

"I'll call you when I land." Her aunt shoved a set of keys into her hands. With a quick peck on the cheek, Aurora waved at her approaching uncle and ducked around a few distant relatives huddled under several black umbrellas on the steps. From the few words she caught, someone thought the tainted past of the late Starr and his troubled daughter served as a hot topic to whisper about. The chilled wind carried faint notes of *one of them* and words like *untrustworthy* and *tainted.*

Anger bubbled in the pit of her stomach until a bitter taste entered her mouth. Not that she wanted to give any excuses, but at least her father had a reason for hating otherworldlies—humans born of both shifter blood and human.

She might only have human hearing, but even the dead could pick up on the shameful tone tossed at her for being a *shifter lover*. Once tainted in the eyes of the high and mighty of her father's inner circles there was no going back. Money didn't make you a decent human being. These people were more savage than the shifters they held prejudice against.

Trying not to catch the tip of her heel on jagged bricks of the walkway, she didn't bother to acknowledge any of the old hens mixed up with a few well-creased suits. No one had time for that crap or the fake sentiments. She risked a glance at her watch as she reached the graveled road.

With a double click, the doors to the Town Car flicked open and she slid in and not a moment too soon. Several trench coats were already weaving through the crowd to catch up. "Sorry." She hit the lock switch and turned over the motor. "Not this time, boys."

Having Starr as a surname and being a top executive assistant for the second highest precious gem mining company made bodyguards one more thing she had to deal with on a regular basis.

But not today. Aurora hit the little green button on her cell phone before the first full ring finished. "Ms.

Donavan's—" she quickly caught her slip. "Excuse me. I apologize. Ms. Starr speaking." Breaking the habit of answering the phone as an *elite* Donovan assistant for one of her father's competitors would take a little bit. A long pause carried over the speakerphone. "Hello? Can I help you?"

"Yes, Ms. Aurora Starr, I'm calling about your travel arrangements." Curt and to the point. Her father's secretary never cracked a smile or, God forbid, exchanged pleasantries.

"Yes, Ms. Chadwell." With the phone tossed to the passenger side, Aurora craned her neck around to check for passing cars, not that there would be many on a single lane cemetery road, but hey, one tended to be a little more careful when the view out the windshield was acres of stone slabs in a variety of sizes.

"I'm calling to confirm your flight times. I have you for an eleven-thirty departure."

How could she forget? "I'll be there. Thank you for the reminder, Ms. Chadwell." With a flick across the smooth glass, she ended the call and stuffed the phone back into her coat pocket, mentally adding a note to pick up something on her trip to smooth the rough edges of her soon-to-be assistant.

Just the thought of dealing with Chadwell on a daily basis made her pulse plummet.

She had one more stop and then she could be on her way. Executing her father's last wishes in secrecy took some finagling, but the end was in sight.

The drive passed in a blur and within minutes of stowing her single carry-on, the skies opened up and drowned out the shrinking skyline of New York City.

CHAPTER TWO

"Home sweet home."

Aurora shut off her rental car and took in the sight of the one town on earth her father vowed she could never return to. Vowed until he lost all color to his face that over his dead body would any kin of his ever return to Claw Ridge, Alaska.

Why he picked it as his final resting place still sat heavy on her mind.

Hard to believe that twenty-four hours ago her surroundings were gray and colorless compared to the postcard worthy view beyond her windshield.

Snow-tipped mountains gave way to a crystal clear sky so blue it made the world look like it glowed with an invisible energy. Cold air filled her lungs and she tilted her head back to catch the first rays of Alaskan sunshine as the midnight sun gave away to morning. As precious as the stones her father pulled from the frozen ground. More so in her opinion, but no board member could pocket that value.

"Hey sweetheart, you lost, or in need of a little help?" A deep craggy voice shattered her moment of Zen. Aurora shot the intruder a sideways glance and returned her attention to the gas pump.

Squinting, she held up a hand to block the rays angled just so to hit her square in the face.

Ash-blond hair caught the rays of morning light momentarily hiding his face. Before she could blink, he towered over her. By then, it was too late to make a fast withdrawal to the safety of her car or the store. He appeared out of nowhere that she could see and covered the distance of the small parking lot in a handful of strides.

She shifted positions and placed the sun at her back. Smeared grease covered most of the coverall, and the grungy orange material looked faded and tattered in places from prolonged use. A small, white logo stood out on the sleeve, marking him as a mechanic from the shop around the corner. He must have been watching to catch her all the way over here.

With a tilt to his head, he performed one of those one-sided elbow leans on the gas pump probably thinking it made all the chicks dig him.

She huffed her surprise as she flipped the lever to the gas pump. "You have to be kidding."As misinformed as he may be, it might have worked if he didn't ooze massive amounts of creepy dude vibes and rock a half-torn wife beater like they weren't standing in on the fringes of the Arctic Circle.

That meant he was shifter. Only they could run around as if it was summer all year long and not be affected. *One that could tear you limb from limb in a blink, just like your mother. You can't trust them.* Aurora forced down her father's voice echoing in the back of her mind.

With him propped up on her gas pump, she had no choice but to reach around him to return the nozzle.

She needed to get going if she had any hopes of making it off the mountain before nightfall. Who knew, if lucky, maybe she'd be out of here before then. Keeping her promise to her aunt might score her a twofer—apple pie AND her award-winning chicken soup.

A girl needed her comforts.

Aurora flipped the lid to her rental car's gas tank closed and stepped around the wall of a man who couldn't find a clue if it were taped to his forehead apparently.

In her line of work, getting bullied by entitled pricks and hit on all in the same hour happened to be another day at the office. "After the week I've had, buster, don't. Just don't." She sliced a hand through the air and put several feet of cracked cement between them.

"Come on, let me make it better." He reached out and caught a strand of her air between his fingers.

Ugh. Aurora stepped back with her hands up. "Look, I'll go my way, you go yours, Gigantor." *Don't antagonize the man, smart-ass.* The lopsided smile that pulled at the corner of his lips made her stomach do a chug and heave.

"You haven't seen big yet, baby." In a sleazy glide he wrapped his hand around his crotch and cupped his bulge.

Seriously? The man had the looks to land any girl, but his method needed an overhaul. Her heartbeat rattled around in her chest and almost made her lose her step as she rounded the trunk of her four-wheel-drive.

Steel fingers wrapped around her upper arm and dragged her close with a yank.

"Look, whoever you are," she threw a hand up between them. "Go find a back alley grizzly girl to play hanky-panky with—I'm definitely not your type."

Beady blue eyes peered down at her as if calculating how far he could push her before the claws came out. His stare bored into her and caused her to slink back.

"How would you know? I happen to be everybody's type, sweetheart. Wait till you get a good long taste."

"Keep dreaming, pal!" God, the man needed a Tic-Tac and a shower. All in that order. She dug her heel into the cement. Raised her opposite arm and shoved her palm into the bridge of his nose before he could make good on his promise with his puckered lips inching closer.

"Surprise! Next time, take a hint."

His grip loosened and she pulled free. "You stupid little bitch." She backtracked, her target the double glass doors of the convenience store and as much space between her and the angered shifter as possible. He could be anything from a fox to a bear, but half of her suspected he would turn into a snake any second.

He raised his hand and she flinched as her boot caught on the raised platform for the gas tanks. But the fated backhand across the cheek never came.

"Unless you want to find yourself answering to the Elder I suggest you get your sorry ass out of my face, Brax. I don't think I need to remind you what happens when you get another strike on your record." Her eyebrows shot up so far they had to be touching her hairline. Her gaze danced between both men and the arrogant smile her new admirer wore swiftly faded to a deep scowl.

Whatever *it* was had to be bad.

Fear filled the creases outlining his lips and eyes. It was plain to see as was the fake bravado he wore like a shield against an alpha werebear. Cold-hearted hatred chilled the air between the men beyond anything Mother Nature could do to an Alaskan winter.

So he was a grizzly?

Brax growled but didn't make a move other than to toss a nasty look filled with cold fury over his shoulder at her. Like she'd planned this all to get him in trouble.

"Keep your woman outta my way." The way he slung out the warning made her spine go rigid. Several seconds slipped by as they watched the hulking man slink back around the corner.

"Are you okay?" Slightly dazed, she momentarily missed the outstretched hand her mirage offered. He couldn't be real. Could he? *Oh get a grip. You knew running into your past lover would happen.* But nothing actually prepared her for the chance encounter.

"I, uh, yeah, I think." Adam fuuurrreeaaking Wylde loomed over her, his thick thighs covered in some sort of bright orange snow gear and the upper half unzipped to hang freely around the waist to reveal his chest wrapped in what had to the tightest shirt ever made in the history of mankind. God, what a chest! Even in the form-fitting, long-sleeved pull over he sported not a detail slipped past her raking gaze. She made sure of it!

Until her gaze landed on his. In that instant, the sunshine, the snow capped mountains and all the heartbreak weighing on her melted away.

Heat rushed into her cheeks and she took his outstretched hand. "What was that guy's problem?"

Adam shook his head and a soft scent of pine lingered between them. As if he spent the dawn hours in the woods and nature clung to him. "The ice bear is a puzzle even to me."

So he was not a grizzly.

Whiskey eyes, warm and inviting, lured her in. She heard him say something, but didn't pay too much attention to it. Two dimples on either side of his cheeks sent a lightning bolt of lust to strike her square in the girly parts.

How crazy. She couldn't help but feel safe. Drawn to the man she hadn't laid eyes on in forever and a day.

She nodded. More than one thing hadn't changed since she'd left the snowy picturesque landscape five years ago.

Gently he took her hand and hauled her up with a little too much force. She lost her balance and stumbled forward. Hands out, she clutched the nearest thing within reach. Wouldn't you know it. Two well-formed pecs were right where her hands landed. She groaned and his eyes turned from whiskey to molten gold in a flash. The throaty growl made her want to taste his lips. All she had to do was lean a little closer...

Had his eyes always been so sexy? So bright?

"Aurora," Adam gruffly whispered in the small space between their lips.

"Sorry." Her breath caught. Did her fingers just flex? Oh God. She yanked her betraying hands back and forced them to stay at her side. Why did she have to pack the one pair of pants that had no pockets!

"I hit my head." She cringed inwardly. Let him know you're off your rocker. Smooth.

She'd lost her damned mind.

Was it too unrealistic to ask for someone to light a match and blow the gas station? A squeaky groan slipped and she took a couple of steps toward her car. Mirth brightened his irises and the firm straight-faced man that played her guardian angel melted into the warm, smiling Adam Wylde she fell in love with when she was the sweet, innocent seventeen-year-old.

Adam Wylde, the grizzly shifter.

"Did your old man make it back with you?" Adam scanned their surroundings looking for a threat of some sort to pop out at him.

Her mind briefly drifted back to the boy barely older than her. In his awkward teenage years he'd been handsome, but never in a thousand years did she think he'd turn out to be so... gorgeous. Not that he knew it from the way he wore the same bright smile and easygoing manner.

"Uh, no. You don't need to worry. It's just me." From one foot to the other she shifted her weight and hoped he didn't dig deeper. Even as a teenager, or youngling as their elder called shifter cubs, Adam had been bigger than the rest of his cousins. Now he towered over her a good half a foot, making her five-five stature feel petite.

Her knees trembled in time with her racing heart. Small lines creased the space between his eyes and her gaze roved over her very impressive mirage. Adam wasn't the boy she remembered. He'd gained weight in all the right places. Once lanky arms and legs now robust with heavily defined muscles.

Finger-length sable hair brushed the collar of his shirt. It was longer than she remembered, but he still rocked out the mussed don't-give-a-damn look, but in a sexy way. Longer strands swept down to brush either side of his face. Not too long, but enough to make her fingers twitch with the urge to touch. She had to admit the man oozed sex appeal without even trying.

Adam looked over her shoulder for the man who'd once cursed him and his people with every fiber of his being. "Sorry to hear that."

She smiled politely, twisting her fingers into a knot to keep them to herself. She doubted it, but she appreciated the sentiment for her sake anyway. "I have to be going. I have a flight to catch. But it was really great seeing you." Aurora bit the inside of her cheek at the lie. If she let him in on her real plans he'd try to stop her.

"Is that so, Aurora Starr?" Adam closed the distance between them. Heat swallowed her up the closer he came and she loved it. Wanted more of him. Was it possible to fall in love at first sight for a second time?

He said her name in a slow drawl with just a hint of gravely inflection that coaxed memories from the deep well she hoped to have drowned them in. Apparently they'd found a life raft and clung on like little pesky nuisances to come back and bite her in the ass when she least expected it. Because what else explained the way her veins flooded with an unsolicited amount of adrenaline as Adam tangled her fingers with his?

Breathe in. Breathe out.

Her face warmed as his eyes came alive with an otherworldly glow. Tingles brushed along her skin as if she didn't have a stitch of clothing on. Steel bands wrapped around her and pulled her deeper until her body flushed against his. One muscle at a time relaxed into his hold. He knotted the length of her ponytail around his hand and angled her lips upward. As that one action held her spellbound, the nerves between her legs throbbed in anticipation. His nostrils flared and the gold specks in his eyes grew danced with energy.

"Carebear, is that you?"

Adam froze as the magick binding them together snapped at the intrusion.

He looked down at her. "This isn't over." Voice thick with emotion, he took a half a pace back and with him the delicious heat he emitted. Unable to break the connection any more than she was, he tightened his fingers around hers.

The look in his gaze connected as if invisible magic twined them together. Her nipples pebbled in the soft confines of her bra at the sinful promise. She pressed her lips together and swallowed.

"It is you! Damn, Adam why didn't you tell me guests were coming?"

Oh God, she couldn't handle two Wylde boys at once. A big diesel rig pulled up behind her. So tied up in the moment she failed to hear the arrival of Adam's brother.

"Everett. She pulled out her handy insta-smile and flashed her pearly whites as she turned on her heel. Braced for impact, in two seconds the middle boy of the Wylde den men had her pinned against him, feet off the ground and squeezing her into a giant bear hug. Whatever they fed these Alaskans made their men iron solid and drool-worthy down to the double dimples. That last one was probably genetic, but damn she'd never seen red plaid look so good on a man.

"She can't breathe, for God's sake. Let the poor girl go."

Everett planted her back on the ground, but didn't let her go. This made his brother scowl deeper.

"I think you may have irritated your brother quite thoroughly." Feeling bold from the big welcome, Aurora tossed a wink at Adam that scored her the classic Adam stare. Hands crossed over his chest and straight line for a mouth. But the golden flecks of his irises still swirled with the same energy as before.

"Damn girl, you're looking fine. New York has been better than just good for you." Everett pulled back from her and placed both hands on her shoulders. Letting out a low whistle, he twirled her around. Shucking the designer shoes for the more practical gear of Alaska, she couldn't help but feel self-conscious over her several layers of sweaters and jeans tucked into her ankle-high boots. It had been a long time since her last winter here.

If Adam frowned any deeper his face would crack.

"Yeah, who knew I had city-girl blood in my veins?" Aurora shared a laugh and another hug from Everett who couldn't seem to believe she was real.

Despite hating the nickname he Christened her with after he and Adam had taken down a bully who'd made fun of her freckles in eighth grade, Aurora smiled. This time for real.

"I see you're still a big flirt, how are you? Have you made any lucky girl Mrs. Wylde yet?"

"I don't know about that, but I've made a few *go* wild if you know what I mean?" Everett waggled his brows and made her laugh. Adam groaned beside her. Aurora tucked a strand of hair behind her ear and dipped her head to hide a giggle.

In a matter of seconds one of her oldest childhood friends brushed away some of the dark gloom from her aching heart.

"Ahem... Playboy here was just leaving."

Everett reached over and tousled her loose hair as if they were still those young kids without a care in the world.

"Not so fast bro." Adam growled, but that didn't seem to slow Everett's roll any. "Listen, Carebear, come on by the house later on. Mom is pulling together a nice meal to celebrate Mira's baby."

Baby? The younger Wylde sister had a baby? "I don't think that's a great idea." Adam shuffled beside her and she caught the stiff look that passed between him and Everett.

"Nonsense. You've been missed in these parts. Dad would love to see you and Mom too. Hell the whole den would love to give you a big hug and see what you've been up to since leaving us."

Adam nailed Everett with a glare at his poor choice of words. Sometimes the filter between his brain and mouth malfunctioned growing up and landed him in some hot water on a few occasions. Apparently it still did.

She placed a hand over Everett's. "It's fine, really."

"No pressure okay, but it would be nice to have you come over." As if stepping right back in without missing a beat, Everett welcomed her back just like that. With Adam, she still walked on thin ice. The instant heat kindled right back up, but walking back into their lives as if nothing happened? That she couldn't do.

A small part of her envied their large, easygoing family. The bond they shared went beyond anything her family ever had for one another.

Beneath heavy lashes she risked a glance at Adam who'd taken a step back from her and crossed his arms like a man that didn't have time for little brothers and old girlfriends. For a moment it looked as if he wanted to push his brother back in the cab of his truck and be rid of him too.

He was right. She'd come here for one purpose.

She flicked away the distraction of the allure Everett painted for her and worked her mouth open to decline.

As if sensing her mental shift, he spoke up.

"Besides, Mom is gearing up for summer solstice too. I think you still know what that means." How could she forget? That had her eyebrows climbing. Mama Wylde's barbecue made the worst of enemies momentarily set aside differences. "If you're going to be around for a while, meet us back at the lodge up on Rum Run Road and we'll head home together."

She smiled at the mention of the town's best unkept secret. Rum Run Road is where the town held their annual knicker run fest. After drinking down a pint of rum all the contestants stripped down to their knickers and raced to the end of the main drag that cut through the heart of downtown. One of the best ways to pass the cold winter and introduce the tourist to the local flavor of crazy.

Home. Neither brother seemed to notice, but that single word made her heart swell. After everything her father said and did to these wonderful people, how could they welcome her with open arms? Everett couldn't know his family would welcome her so graciously.

He bent to place a chaste kiss to her cheek before pegging Adam with a pair of gloves he pulled from his back pocket. "Saddle up man, we've had an avalanche on the backside of Base One. Rangers are already scouting the area and have called in the additional support. You and me are playing air taxi too."

Base One. "How bad?" She let the question slip out as if she was only asking out of fear for the possibly injured people. She cared for them, hoped they were all okay and could make it down in one piece and breathing, but if the back passage was closed, she'd be trapped here with Adam until she could do what she came here to do. That was beyond dangerous.

"Don't know. It wasn't anyone we took up. People fool enough to be back there alone, sorry to say it, has it coming."

Adam rubbed a hand over the back of his neck and nodded as Everett pulled back to the truck to give them some space.

Adam turned to her. "Wait for me. Don't go anywhere. We need to talk. Wait for me. Please?"

Damn. His eyes pleaded with her and it cut her deeper than she thought possible. She swallowed and bit at her inner lip. Pine invaded her senses and whiskey eyes filled her vision. He stood so close. Warm fingers cupped her face, and he held her attention the second his fiery gaze locked on hers with enough heat to ignite something so deep within her that no one had touched in forever. Since him.

"I'll pick you up from the lodge." Of course he knew where she would be with only one place open to tourists.

No question in his tone, no plea for obedience. Simply stated, Adam expected her to obey. She braced herself. Air caught in her lungs, refusing to budge. He lowered his head just as Everett honked his horn. She clenched her hands at her side to keep from holding him where he stood. "Wait for me." His words brushed against her ears and reached deep inside to stir up more than emotions. He conjured up something else she didn't quite understand. There was no stopping the warm flush that consumed her from head to toe.

Damn him.

Aurora watched the tail lights of their truck disappear around the corner of the gas station. Adam Wylde knew better than to turn his alpha werebear loose on her.

CHAPTER THREE

*C*limb the damn mountain.
Spread her father's ashes.
Find what her father sent her for.
Be gone before anyone can come looking for her.

Namely Adam.

Aurora mentally ticked off the four points. Six hours ago in the shower of her tiny lodge room it had sounded like a perfectly solid plan.

Now her heart did a little jig just thinking about his warm touch and kissable lips. The way his hand felt holding hers. Gentle yet strong. Instead of stiff and damn near frozen solid like hers.

Every second that passed the once blue skies turned a mucky gray.

Snow. And, by the looks of it, a lot.

Nailing one out of three on her to-do list was pathetic. She held several self-titled degrees in how to escape assigned bodyguards yet couldn't manage to keep a low profile for more than two hours? In her defense, she still had time to make her great escape. She only needed to spread her father's ashes and haul ass back to Fairbanks and the nearest airport before any of the six Wylde brothers caught on to her plan. If one thing they did well it was work together when they had a plan and if one wanted something they all teamed up. And one thing she did not want was to be the center of their attention when they had a plan.

"Why did it have to be him? Why Adam?"

She groaned, not that anyone would hear her halfway up the backside of a mountain.

Cold fingers of regret ran the length of her spine.

He smelled so good. Like Ivory soap with a mixture of pine and snow. She loved the freshness of snow.

Echoes of the past jolted her out of the black funk that had dogged her for the past few days—going on what felt like forever—in the time it took to say hello. Talk about bad timing.

When he'd uttered her name in that deep voice of his, almighty Thor's hammer would do less damage to her self-control. Another second and she may have done something unacceptable. Like tossing herself into his arms and feeling him up. God, he must really pity her.

Did it count if she rolled her eyes at her own actions? Could she have been any more obvious? She dug her toes into the firmly packed snow and hauled herself belly first over a freshly felled tree the size of a horse.

All she had to do was make it another couple of hours, pull off some highly evasive maneuvers, maybe a few Hail Mary's and make like Mick Jaggar back to the lodge. Hell, screw that. She'd call from the airplane and have her stuff forwarded back to New York.

No. That wouldn't work. That nosy Mr. Kravitz would rat her out and give anyone and everyone in town her address.

No. She could pick up more panties and bras. Losing her brand new laptop burned, though.

Aurora shoved aside her scattered thoughts and refocused on her task. Two hours had passed since the encounter and from the looks of it, no one had followed her.

"That's a good sign, Starr." Then why did she feel disheartened?

Eye on the prize and making good time, she scanned the horizon. Only another hundred yards or so.

Loose rocks shifted under Aurora's weight and shook any remaining garbled thoughts away.

Focus.

One wrong move and she'd be in a bad way this high up. The so-called path she managed was more of a guideline that led to a secret lookout point tourists didn't know about than a real path. No climbing harnesses needed, but it was still a long way over the side if you managed to piss off the wrong gods.

With agile fingers, she easily caught hold of the rock face and repositioned her footing before pushing another few steps on the narrow path. Her hand shot out in reflex. With gloved fingers, she found large crevices for leverage and hauled herself forward on the steady incline before it fell away to reveal vast open sky and a sea of snow-tipped treetops is various shades of misty white to deep, lumberjack green.

Puffy vapor billowed out with every heavy exhale.

"Starr's Point." Named after her father before she was born for discovering it.

Thanks to him, climbing was in her blood and truth be told, she missed the challenge more than she realized before now.

Looking over the vast forest spread out below, the white wonderland would soon be lush and vibrant with summer. Aurora couldn't help but take a moment. She'd missed this. The peace and tranquility. Such a stark contrast to the constant chaos of the New York City streets.

Not many knew of the easy way around to the point. Or maybe they preferred the harder straight up and over approach. Which she normally did, but there were enough mountains to climb in her life at the moment—she didn't need to literally add another.

Sharp winds cut around the jagged rockface and tore into the smallest of openings in her thick winter coat. She bent and tucked into the blustery weather. Hunkered close to the ground, she moved away from the ledge and closer to the medium-sized rocks that rimmed a section of blackened stone that normally served as a source of heat and cooking. As a young girl and through her teenage years her dad and mom had cooked several summertime meals here. Her favorite had been homegrown corn from Mrs. Wylde's garden and her dad's grilled fish. If she concentrated, she could still smell the lemon zest.

Tears welled along the rims of her eyes. Back then things had been simpler. Back before the attack stole her mother away and drove her father to bury himself in nothing but building an empire. His heart turned to solid stone that made the diamonds he mined look soft in comparison.

Her mother had loved the outdoors. With their log cabin and large expanse of property backed up to the west side of the Arctic National Wildlife Refuge she would disappear for hours until one day she didn't come back.

Desperate, her father had called in every law enforcement agency, but after forty-eight hours they'd failed to find her. It had been the elder of the Wylde Den that had found her body mauled by a rogue werebear.

A throaty roar echoed off the walls of the two mountains Starr Point settled between. As if her thoughts conjured a reverberating memory from the rocks themselves.

She stood, heart pounding against her sternum. Wild ideas of a werebear hunting her down overshadowed her thoughts for a split second. She had to stop letting her father's fears be her own.

Another roar split the eerie silence. It had to be the rescue team out looking for the hikers.

To the right of where she stood, the ledge extended into the mountainside a few feet before tucking under an overhang that led to a small secluded den.

Apparently winter had hit hard this year. Layers of snow partially buried the entire path on her way up, and it plastered against the rocks in a way that a baker would ice a cake.

Ominous clouds draped across the once blue horizon. Fat flakes swirled in the air and caught in the loose strands of her ponytail. With deft fingers she popped the double-hooked clasps on her bag. She didn't have long. Kneeling beside the pit, Aurora slipped her flashlight from her bag as she stood to make her way into the dark den.

"Why the hell did I have to make a promise to him?" She knew better, yet the plea his eyes held tore her heart out.

"Because you're weak, Aurora Starr," she quipped to her own question.

Weak because in that one moment all his past transgressions against her vanished in a poof and all she saw before her was a man desperate for one last moment with his daughter.

After hours of talking, he slipped away from her.

"So, here we are, now it's your turn, Father." Aurora tightened her grip on her satchel. "You promised answers for a peaceful resting place close to mom. The ball's in your court."

What answers he thought she needed to find still puzzled her. Whatever he wanted to tell her he'd insisted could only be found here.

Aurora pressed her hands to her face and inhaled a long steadying breath.

Holding the satchel that carried her father's ashes, she leaned in. "Any time would be nice. Feel free to toss out a divine clue of what I should be looking for."

Flashlight in hand, she entered the den. Shafts of light lanced down in crisscross patterns through the slots cutting through the cavern's ceiling. Mother Nature had created a few sunroofs and the added light helped her see. Standing in the mouth of the cave, Aurora bounced the light from side to side. Small crates were stacked along the far wall covered in what looked like a tarp. People, probably the teenagers of Claw Ridge, still visited the point. But not for a few months at least judging from the tattered, worn material.

She pushed into the small opening that led deeper into the cavern, passed the initial wide chamber and into a place the cold wind couldn't follow.

In a few steps she kneeled by the crates and thumbed through the contents. Nothing stood out.

If she wanted to make it down before the sun dipped to the horizon for the night she had to hurry. Heat juiced her blood and she returned to the entrance. He'd said she'd find it here, that all she had to do was look hard enough. Only, she wished she knew what it was. Frustration tore a gargled scream from her throat.

"Why can't you ever just tell the truth? Why! Why the riddles and games?" She kneeled in the growing amount of snow, placing the bag by her knee.

"Perfect! This was such a terrible idea." She pounded a fist into the snow and let the horror and anger of coming all the way out here for nothing feed the drive behind her force. He fostered such a soul-deep hatred for the shifters, why the hell would he send her back into the heart of their territory? Maybe the medicines had messed with his mind? Maybe she needed meds.

She'd come a long way and risked more than her neck to play some kind of game.

Anger forced her to her feet in a rush, and she stormed to the ledge. She had to be the biggest fool. With jerky movements she gathered her bag. Thunder pounded against the earth. "What the heck is that?" Crouched low she scanned the horizon. Since when did thunder come from the ground?

Aurora turned a one-eighty as fear gripped her in its ironclad fist. Her throat closed the second a startled scream worked its way up her windpipe.

Her head jerked around and she froze in place. "BEAR!"

CHAPTER FOUR

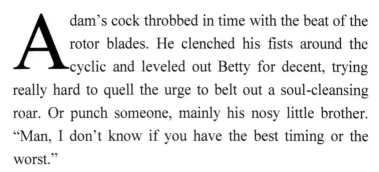

Adam's cock throbbed in time with the beat of the rotor blades. He clenched his fists around the cyclic and leveled out Betty for decent, trying really hard to quell the urge to belt out a soul-cleansing roar. Or punch someone, mainly his nosy little brother. "Man, I don't know if you have the best timing or the worst."

"Probably all a matter of perspective." Everett's retort crackled over their closed coms system. "You didn't tell her, did you?"

Red tinted his vision. That perpetual *nothing ever bothers me* stupid, little smirk was parked on his brother's face just to taunt him. He knew damn well it irritated the hell out of him on normal days. Today, it down right made him see red.

"How could I? And why the hell did you do that?" Only in the last fifteen minutes of their flight did the turbulence level out enough for him to nail his brother with a glare that could melt polar ice caps. He needed more time to formulate a plan to tell her that her father had reached out to him a few days ago. Her being here meant the man he once hated had passed.

Being thrown together with Aurora before he could get a handle on the scrambled emotional mess he called a brain sat like a pound of rocks in his gut.

"What?" Paying attention to Betty's controls, Adam maneuvered the chopper between the sea of pines and touched down in the designated spot big enough to accommodate the size of their bird.

Perfect every time.

Back to glaring at Everett, Adam flicked the dial on the radio to call in their position. "Home base, this is Big Bear, we've landed and are on site. Base One will be in contact. Have paramedics on standby."

"Copy that, Big Bear. We'll be here. And guys, be careful up there. This looks bad." Their kid sister's ominous warning of the approaching storm took a little air out of his sails.

Base One was just the beginning and they had a lot of ground to cover in a short amount of time. From here they had to hike around the base of Claw Ridge to reach where the climbers were last seen by the patrolling rescue crew with boots already on the ground.

"Playing coy doesn't suit a grizzly, Ev. You know damn well the more time I spend with her the worse off we all are."

"Look, you told me yourself you were expecting her. You don't get answers by keeping people at a distance. Mating season or not. From what you say, her father called you for the favor and not the other way around. The least you're owed, hell we're all owed, are some answers."

"It's not just about that." Damn. If shit would just stop happening, he could figure out what the hell he wanted to say to her that didn't start with *I wanna fuck you until we both can't go anymore.* Those things required finesse, more than what he had available at the moment.

"I love Aurora like a kid sis, but you, brother, need to face your mating season head-on or it'll take you down. Try ignoring that."

He shot a glare at his brother.

"Yeah, I can see it written all over your face and the heat. It's already started, hasn't it?"

"How would you know?"

"I have eyeballs."

"Let's see what you'll do when it comes for you."

"Nah, that ain't happening. But back to you. Don't think I haven't seen you wallow around in your own self-doubt for the last week solid."

"That's none of your business."

"And that's not counting the last five-plus years," his brother plowed on.

In unison they performed their routine systems check and powered down Betty.

"Hey guys, so when did Aurora get back?"

Adam froze. What the hell? He bared his teeth and gave a long drawn-out growl as he flicked the coms off back to home base. Now his sister and the whole of fucking headquarters knew his business and all Everett could do was grin like a silly cub.

"You did that on purpose."

"I needed backup."

Everett may have a point, but like hell he'd feed his brother's ego. "That's low, wait until I tell mom. What kind of brother brings in the little sis for back up?"

"A smart one, that's who!" Everett reached across and gave him a slap on the shoulder that sent his grizzly into ass-kicking mode. Adam unstrapped himself from the cockpit and launched himself from the door. It was that or risk throwing a left hook into the other man's jaw.

He swiveled his gaze as his brother crossed the front of the chopper shaking his head, wearing that damn smirk. He took long strides, the snow slowing him down, when a raven-haired woman popped her head out of the tent twenty yards up the small incline to another naturally leveled area. She flashed a sweet smile and his brother froze as if caught in a spell. *Well, I'll be damned.* He knew that look. Not on his brother, but he recognized smitten when he saw it. Every piece of that particular puzzle snapped into place, but one. How did he not know about this before now?

"Never my ass."

Ignoring his jab, Everett's face lit up with an animated expression he'd never witnessed before. Interesting.

Thunder rumbled an eerie warning and caught his attention. Eyes locked on the skyline, he swore under his breath. The fucking weatherman had it all wrong again, but any veteran of Alaska could tell the second the weather turned for the worse. It didn't make any sense. Why would anyone be out here with a storm this size rolling in?

Experience had everyone making double time to find the lost hikers and get them off the mountainside in time enough to hunker down back at the headquarters of Wylde Excursions. Or that was the plan if the missing hikers were still living.

Blood rushed in his ears. Aurora was going to be the death of him. Icy wind whipped around the edges of the tent and smacked him in the face. She served as a lethal combination to his grizzly and he needed to focus. Until now, he never cursed his shifter genes. Not when she was yanked out of his life because of what he was and not when her father used his money to bury their family business before uprooting. But today, for one split second he couldn't help but think about the *what ifs* of their shared past.

One thing he hadn't counted on the second their eyes connected was his bear claiming her as their mate. He figured he had another month before he had to deal with that particular side of his nature. Time enough to deal with her, as he'd promised her father. She'd be long gone before his season kicked in and he could go through with *not* finding a mate.

Adam groaned and strode forward, sinking to his knees in soft snow until he reached the tent. There had been at least a foot of the sugary powder covering already loosely packed snow from the way his foot sank in with little resistance.

A recipe for disaster. They set patrol up for this very reason. Whoever let these fools back here to hike should be arrested. When they returned to town, he'd have a few details to nail down, but he had an idea of who the hikers were and if his inside info panned out, the town of Claw Ridge was on the verge of a big shift. Not to mention what would happen to Wylde Excursions. But first, he needed to fact check.

Sharp stings pierced the cavity of his chest and shot straight to his heart. Adam clutched at the searing burn. Heat of the mating season slowly seeped into his veins like an IV drip with each thump of his heart. He didn't know how long he had before all hell broke loose, but he needed to make sure he wasn't anywhere near her when it happened. When the heat of his grizzly took over, any rational thinking shifted to pure adrenaline-infused instinct. His human and bear mind shifted together with a single goal: find and claim their mate.

A mating always involved hours of sweaty sex and intense orgasms. Hours alone with Aurora...

All these layers. He pulled at his collar. God, they were suffocating him. A flush of sweat broke out over his entire body, dragging a wave of chills in its wake.

Sharp, talon-like claws tore at the thin gauzy layer of membrane that separated him from his bear. His animal stretched, pawed to be freed.

Adam felt the urge to turn around and seek out the little green-eyed temptress just to prove to himself he could resist the instinct hardwired into his brain.

The thrill of the hunt gunned his adrenaline. He wouldn't have to look far. She'd strolled back into his life and served herself up on a silver platter complete with the sweetest damn face he'd ever seen.

Jealousy never occurred to him. Maybe he never felt strongly enough for a woman, but when he caught that lowlife Brax making a move, his world zeroed in on making a kill. Only by the skin of his own hide did he manage not to pulverize the fucking misplaced ice bear where he stood.

They'd done him a favor accepting him into their den. Grizzlies and ice bears didn't mix. Tempers flared and usually kept the species apart, but the Elder felt obligated to help a fellow otherworldly in need. He didn't share the sentiment. Only the thought of seeing any kind of fear on Aurora's face had kept him in check. Repeating history wouldn't do him any favors.

Adam felt his control slip a sliver. He'd risk getting close to her one more time for another hit of her alluring, cock-teasing scent.

Adam braced his thick-soled boots deeper into the snow for a better grip just in time to take a gust of wind brutal enough to lift him a few inches if he were any less of a man.

Son of a bitch.

His back teeth ground together when his grizzly shivered.

He stepped into the makeshift home base and all eyes locked on him. "How bad is it, Chief?" He shook hands with the leader of the Mountain Rescue who also doubled as the Firehouse Chief. In a town this small almost everyone doubled up on something.

Topography maps covered the table between them. "The avalanche took place in this section of the mountain."

His fears were slowly becoming a reality. The west sector bordered Aurora's father's land and stretched into no mans land along the base of the mountain. No outsider would know that, though.

Son of a bitch. He should have been paying attention to the radio this morning and not daydreaming about Irish, green eyes, sweet honey, and all the luscious curves of Aurora Starr. Each fucking heartbeat pumped his system with another dose of heat until his air supply shut off.

"Man, you okay?" Everett clapped him on the back. He offered up a weak smile to help ease the worry lines already cutting deep ridges into Everett's forehead.

"Let's go." Adam broke away from the crowd as everyone exited the tent.

"Fire this off if you find them before we do." Chief handed him a flare gun and nodded.

"Copy that."

"We have a little over six hours of real daylight left to find the hikers. We'll take the south side while you Wylde boys take the north."

He nodded once. Fine by him.

"Everett, I'll head up to Starr point and scout out to see if they made it clear. You take the bottom." Everett gave a two finger salute and tossed a two-way over to him.

Static played over the radios before settling in on a station they shared with the other team members. In situations like this, time was crucial and teamwork meant lives saved.

Adam shuffled his climbing gear over his shoulder and secured the straps around his waist. Team one took the southern route and already had rounded the bend out of sight.

To his left a vast amount of pines served as a barrier between the town and any avalanches that could possibly strike. To his right a vast sea of sparkling powder stretched out before him. Ask anyone north of the Arctic Circle and they'd tell you a million and one stories about the grizzlies of Alaska. How the Draeonians of the old world, the first otherworldlies to discover the power of the ley lines, destined the Wylde's souls as werebears because their spirits were too strong for a human's life. Not even the werewolves could harness the power of the werebear.

"Hey guys," a newcomer's voice came in over the two-way.

His brother responded. "Come in, Pepper."

Adam grinned. So that was her name. His brother would be mated by the end of the season. The poor sap was too much in denial to see it.

"The weather station just radioed in. The guy says two hours tops before total whiteout."

That narrowed their window by a hell of a lot.

That was his cue. He wasn't leaving this mountainside until he had something to show for their efforts. God, he hoped it wasn't with body bags.

His grizzly stretched and growled for the hunt.

"Copy that." Adam hooked the radio onto his backpack and turned to his brother.

"Be safe." Everett clasped his arm and pulled him in until their foreheads touched. A strong family connection tied den members together and it pulsed between them like a low rhythmic heartbeat. "Be wild!" He tossed out a sly grin and one last squeeze to their clasped hands.

He held up his radio. "Hit me up if you find them. I'll do the same."

"See you on the flip side."

His brother started his descent as he started the climb. Finally alone, he made quick calculations. On two legs, it would take him hours to scour the expanse he needed to cover. The hikers didn't have that long. If they were missed by the avalanche and had any sense, they would have made their way to the nearest protection from the storm. Starr point was their best bet, and his. Carrying his supplies in his mouth would be a bitch, but he didn't have much of a choice. With swift choppy movements he tossed off his pack and boots. Next his pants joined the pile and the rest of his gear, and then he stowed everything away in his pack or tied it to the exterior.

Damn.

Strong gusts whipped around the side of the ledge. He sucked air out of surprise and fell to his knees.

Kneeling, he let the magic of the werebear take over. Heat infused his muscles from the force of his shift.

Fresh snow, pine, and the approaching storm. Every scent more alluring than the next. He loved the wild, brutal world he and his den family called home for the last eighty-plus years.

Bones cracked and fur replaced skin in a sweeping blur.

Human fused with bear and through his beast's eyes, everything came into crystal clear focus. In one swoop he gathered his pack between his teeth and ran. Power surged through his muscles and fear pushed him harder. Beneath his weight snow crunch and his paws punched through the fresh powder now coming down harder.

Werebears were known for their tenacity and calculating moves. The US government caught on quick after the truth of shifters got out a handful of decades back. Within a few years Uncle Sam drafted shifters of all kinds into their ranks to form platoons depending on their strengths. His beast's amped-up instincts caught and sorted every scent, labeling them local or foreign. One stood out among the many. Honey. Or at least that's how his bear read the sweet nectar that whipped along the wind.

He took a bend in the trail with a little more force than necessary. Snow shifted and he extended his claws for traction.

Adam dodged a low-hanging branch and made short work of passing a felled tree covering the path.

Flurries of snow spiraled in the air on a stiff ribbon of wind, bringing with it the smell of Aurora.

He stumbled and took a nosedive into a snow drift. What the hell? It couldn't be! Didn't that woman know how to listen?

Big, fat flakes fell harder and faster, several hitting him square on the snout.

From the east a low, rumbled boom cracked through the sounds of the storm. A single flash of light caught his eye from the west.

They'd found them. A part of him eased, but he couldn't rest.

Vibrations rumbled and fed into his paws. Something was wrong.

Fear pushed him up the back trail to Starr Point faster than he'd ever moved before. Felled trees, snow drifts... nothing slowed him down. The farther he went the stronger the scent. Every few feet the path became more precarious for a grizzly of his size and the damn jagged rocks pierced the underside of his paws. He pushed harder. Each stab forced him to focus and forget the cold seeping into his fur.

The rumbling grew louder.

Avalanche.

His heart stopped cold. Without breaking stride, he launched the full weight of his grizzly over the ledge. His gaze shot from side to side until he spotted her. Panic ebbed.

There she was. Safe.

The fist metal band clamping around his heart released.

Movement above her caught his acute gaze. His attention flashed between her shocked expression and a mountainside that appeared to be shifting above them.

Fear and panic collided with the adrenaline in his blood and tasted like a shot of acid down the back of his throat. He opened his mouth in warning, but only a bellowed roar came out.

Son of a... no time to shift. His focus narrowed to her vivid green eyes as they pierced his and the same fear he felt mirrored back from the human kneeling over a pile of snow. Thunder penetrated the ground beneath him. Eyes wide, he did the only thing a two-ton bear could do.

CHAPTER FIVE

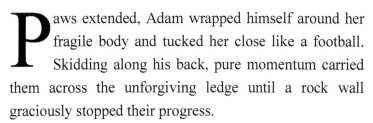

P aws extended, Adam wrapped himself around her fragile body and tucked her close like a football. Skidding along his back, pure momentum carried them across the unforgiving ledge until a rock wall graciously stopped their progress.

He roared in protest. That would hurt for a while. Never mind, he could take the pain. Rumbling continued for another thirty seconds or so before cutting off the main source of light and their only exit.

This just went from bad to worse. The sun already dipped close to the horizon. In another half hour, it would be dusk.

With snow covering the slits in the stone ceiling, darkness fell over them.

Adam stiffened when the bundle in his arms flailed. Elbows, knees, fists and kitten claws.

Mmm. Sexy. A right hook to the ribs, or was that another knee, forced out a huff of air.

Every weapon the woman had she used. Small, muffled grunts and moans brought on other ideas and sounded like angels and bells to his ears. He wanted to shred her clothing with his bare teeth and ravish her until she gave herself up to him.

Palms pressed against his massive, furry chest, her fingers began to tighten around large clumps as she pushed up. Wide-eyed and flushed with anger, Aurora looked down at him and his heart clamored before coming to an abrupt stop.

"You big brute. You oaf. What the hell was that? You big overbearing..." Fury, rage, fear... it all rushed at him and worked its way into her words enough she didn't realize her surroundings. Or the fact she pounded her fists into a grizzly ten times her size.

Now this was the Aurora he remembered. A fiery woman with a sassy mouth that tempted him closer for a taste. Adam shook her loose and pushed to all fours, effectively bumping Aurora to her plush little ass and ending her tirade of expletives. He kinda liked it when she got all worked up, but she needed to conserve her energy. God, why had she left the safety of town?

No telling how long they would be here. Her lips thinned and she stared back at him, her brows pinched together with a frown.

She scoffed, but he doubted she could feel anything given how many layers of pants she had to have on under her outer snowsuit. Come to think of it, how the hell did she even move in that many layers? He made a mental note to ask her as he peeled off each and every stitch of clothing. And he would. Undress her that was. His bear was hungry for a taste of his mate. His bear growled.

Adam stood over Aurora and puffed a hot blast of air in her direction before he pushed his massive weight through the narrow entrance leading deeper into the den. Or at least that had been his plan. Had it gotten smaller since their last time up here?

Seconds later energy flowed over him and the cold wrapped around him. Grizzly shifters ran several degrees hotter than humans and even other otherworldly shifters. Springtime in Alaska was like full-on winter for the lower forty-eight and the bitter cold shrugged off killed mortals. It would do the same to Aurora if he didn't find a way to protect her.

But not him. The fierce need to mate singed his insides and cranked up his internal dial to hellish levels. Right about now, he welcomed the chill and brisk jump to his adrenaline.

He turned abruptly and caught her off-guard as she went to follow him.

"Are you okay? Did you get hurt?" he offered up cautiously, taking a step closer. He knew he needed to get her deeper into the den away from the ice wall at their back, but he couldn't take his eyes off of her. Couldn't pull away.

As much as he tried, he couldn't break the mesmerizing hold as she locked her gaze on him. Like honey to his senses, she lured him closer, whether she knew it or not. This close to mating season she played havoc with his senses. If he continued, there would be no holding back from going fucking crazy in lust for her until he had her back in his bed and coming every which way he could think of. And wearing his mark.

He bared his teeth with a smile, silently loving the way her attention darted between his parted lips and bare chest.

Irritated or not, the lust that swirled around them and brushed against his senses told a story of its own. Her gaze riveted farther south and his cock twitched under her heated attention.

"Oh, God. Your clothes. You need something to wear. You'll freeze. Although, from the looks of it nothing *on* you..." Aurora paused midsentence long enough to draw her eyes to his, "...looks affected by the cold." She simply crossed her arms as if to keep from reaching out, and it made him want to pin her against the wall and see if she still tasted like honey in the springtime.

He sniffed the air. Even through the thick material of her suit she had zipped up tight around her neck, he could scent her arousal.

"You feel it too, don't you?" She could try to hide it, but beneath the ire she fostered for him, something else simmered.

"I don't feel anything but cold."

His hand shot out and captured a wisp of hair that fell loose around her heart-shaped face to brush against her plumps lips. Gently, as not to spook his snow bunny, Adam traced the back of his knuckles along her jaw, tipped her head up and breathed in the deep sigh she released.

"Liar," he accused in the same hushed tone he remembered always affected her.

Fire blazed in her eyes and it mirrored the mating heat that burned in him. An inch, maybe less, and he could have her lips pressed against his. Her body moving over him, his tongue delving within the warm lushness of her delectable mouth.

She would reject him, though. Like she had the last time he stood this close and begged her not to leave him.

"Are you going to eat me with your eyes or are you going to kiss me, Adam Wylde?" Her words came out breathy and raspy with need. How many nights had he dreamed of her saying his name one last time? Masturbated to the vision of her cemented in his memories?

He glided closer. She'd lost weight since he'd seen her last by the way her cheeks hollowed as she spoke. He adored her ample, feminine curves perfect for his larger size and loved how she molded against his body. She wasn't taking care of herself the way a mate would care for her.

He would fix that.

Never while loving a woman had he spilled himself by simply kissing her. With Aurora, he was bordering the edge of that particular experience.

Wedging his thigh between her legs, he caught her waist with one hand and hauled her close with his other pressed to the back of her head.

She would leave again, but not without knowing the truth. Knowing that they were intended as mates.

Gasps and moans melted into his mouth as he claimed her plump, parted lips. Heaven. Sweet, delicious fucking Heaven. The first taste of divinity after five years of tasteless fruit nearly brought him to his knees.

Soft palms pressed into his chest. Feather-light touches trailed down his chest. As though she were relearning the contours of his body, Aurora slowly mapped each scar that marred his chest she knew and a few new ones.

Everything clicked and their surroundings melted away. Adrenaline jacked up his heart rate and hammered against the wall of his chest. Instinct drove the need of the mating heat through his veins until he couldn't think, only act.

With nimble fingers, he slipped the elastic band that held her long masses of sable hair away from her face and relished the way the silken strands slipped through his fingers. She'd grown it out. He tightened his grip around her thick, luscious hair and sank deeper into his siren's heady taste.

Liquid spilled from the tip of his dick to wet his abdomen. With the softest of touches, she glided a single finger up the length of his thickened cock and swirled the spilled liquid. Steel bands wrapped around his gut and it took all he had not to rip her clothes off and fuck her long and hard.

For a fragile second, just one, he wanted to fall to his knees and beg her to stay.

He ground his back teeth and let his head fall back, breaking their kiss. As each of her fingers encased his length, the tighter the cords in his neck drew. Damn, she was killing him. All he could think about was dipping his cock between her legs and coating his shaft with her juices. If she stroked him from tip to base one more time it was over.

Need boiled over. His grizzly clawed at the thin shroud that separated him from his beast. With every second she touched him the neural connection of the mating bond shared between two destined mates grew stronger. The rhythm of her feelings mingled with his until he couldn't tell his from hers.

Fuck her. Claim her. Mark her.

Instinct fogged over the last of his thoughts.

"Don't." He reached between them, eyes squeezed shut. "Not unless you're willing to take me, Aurora." Damn. She robbed every last coherent thought from him. "You want that? You want me to fuck you and take everything away from you, because I'm ready?" Arms stretched out, he offered himself to her.

In mere seconds he witnessed Aurora blink back the heat and longing until uncertainty clouded her eyes.

"I didn't think so."

Her fingers still wrapped around his pulsating cock.

Frustration tore from him, and he pulled away with a deep growl reverberating off the walls. Maybe it would loosen the damn ice wall that held them locked in here and they could get off this fucking mountain. Being this close to her killed him every minute he couldn't have her.

Ire knotted deep in the pit of his stomach. He shoved his discomfort down with a tight grip and straightened to his full height. Peering down at his little snow bunny all dressed in white, he spoke slowly.

"I see nothing has changed, sweetheart." Looking at her, he reached out and thumbed the red blush that stained her cheeks. She wore her heartbreak on her sleeve, and it tore a growl from him. Why did she let the past rule her happiness now?

"And why would it? Last I checked you're still a werebear and I'm still human." The need in her voice broke through, but her words served as an impenetrable wall.

"That's your father speaking. Not you. Or it didn't use to be."

Human, shifter, witch, hell, even vampire. To Adam it didn't matter where you came from. Love was just that—love. Nothing else mattered. Then again, he grew up in the new world only a few years after the otherworldlies showed themselves to mankind. Maybe humans needed longer to process the truth of there being another species out there besides theirs?

"Tell me, has that changed, Aurora?" He stroked the tip of her chin and brought her gaze level with his. "Why did you leave without saying goodbye? After what we shared, I deserved that much." He walked them back until he had her pinned to the stone wall of the den and slid between her thighs.

"We were young."

"And?" Lowering his head, Adam inhaled as he ran his nose from her breasts to her mouth for emphasis. "You know now as you did back then, that we belong together." Hands pinned above her head he looked into her eyes. "Can't exactly lie about that, can you? Answer me, do you feel the call?"

Her gaze darkened. "You know why I left. After Mom died..." She turned her face away and let her words trail off on a huff without answering him. "I'm not going to argue with you, Adam."

"It's like a thousand wires of electricity tapping into every blood cell in your body and pumping your libido with amazing amounts of adrenaline."

Her lashes brushed against the tops of her cheeks, "Yes."

He intertwined their fingers and drew her hands close to rest on his chest. "No one is arguing, sweetheart."

She turned back to face him. "You're right, you know. Father pulled us out of here after the rangers found Mom's body so fast I didn't have a choice. I was barely eighteen. What would you have me do?" In the darkness, his heightened vision picked up the slight smile she tried to hide the pain behind. But he saw through the faux bravado.

"Fight my father?"

Adam stood there, silently staring down at her, and inhaled softly. Maybe it was time to take off the kid gloves? "No, Aurora. Fight *for* your mate."

CHAPTER SIX

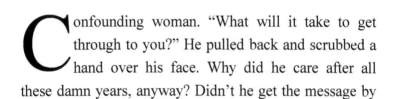

Confounding woman. "What will it take to get through to you?" He pulled back and scrubbed a hand over his face. Why did he care after all these damn years, anyway? Didn't he get the message by now?

"You're making me crazy with your scent." It already burrowed so deep in his brain he'd never be rid of it. Wearing patience ate at his resolve and he tore a hand through his hair. She didn't want him. More so, she didn't want his werebear all because of her damn father.

A muscle ticked in his jaw and he turned away so she couldn't see the war she created inside him. Damn straight. His territory. His mountain. His mate.

He shook his head and silenced the voice of his grizzly which was hard to do with the taste of her lingering on his lips and his cock pulsating.

"Is that a bad thing?"

The possessive need climbed out of the tightly locked box he'd locked it away in five years ago with a vengeance. Stronger than he'd ever felt it before.

"Depends." By the way her eyebrow twitched, he could tell she expected more. When he didn't give it, she produced a skinny flashlight and turned on her heel.

A growl of annoyance slipped before he could catch himself.

"We both know why I can't be your mate." White light filled the four-foot circumference of the small entryway. All stone on one side with a wall of ice and snow on the other. The similarities to their current situation didn't slip by him.

"You mean, being a grizzly's mate isn't good enough for the Starr bloodline." He caught a flash of regret but pushed on anyway. "Wouldn't want to sully the royal family and all."

True Aurora style, her cheeks filled with a bright red blush and her lower lip tucked sideways when she got angry. He missed that little detail.

Adam cocked a brow and crossed his arms over the expanse of his chest.

His little snow bunny looked lovely all ticked off. Good. Maybe that would cut through her denial. Bare-ass naked wasn't how he pictured having this argument, but he could see a few benefits of lowering her defenses with his current situation. Adam raised his arms and crossed them over his chest. Her light followed his movements and then explored farther south.

Low lighting didn't bother him, but he knew she had to struggle to see. Or she really was trying hard not to look down the length of his body despite her raking the light over him from head to toe more than once since their kiss.

Both options would explain the deep creases of concentration between her eyes and the immense waves of anxiety rolling off her with enough power to choke him.

"Can't you... you know?" She made a gesture with her hand to signal the shift between bear and human. As tempting as it was to leave her floundering for words, he stepped in.

"Go all grizzly and punch through the snow?"

"There's gotta be a way out of here, Adam?"

"Not that easy. Hell, I really wish it were."

"Why not? You break through, we can get outta here and go on our merry way."

"The last thing I want to do is hold you here. God forbid, right? But who knows how thick this is. There could be more people below. If I cause a bigger avalanche, it could bury them alive. We're safe here. You're safe." He stepped closer and settled his hands on either shoulder. "I know this mountain better than anyone. After the storm passes, my brother will come for us Probably no later than sunrise. And with him he'll raise an army if need be to get us out."

"Are you sure? How does he even know where we are?"

Adam tipped her chin up just to see her emerald eyes on him. "Trust me. He's good at his job. I lost the two-way, but he knows where I was headed and our gear is equipped with trackers for this very reason. He'll be here as soon as he can."

"For our sakes, I hope."

"What has you so worried?"

"The fact that we have no water. No food and no source of heat is kinda worrisome, wouldn't you say."

"I had food in my pack. And I am the heat source. " He turned back to the entrance and looked back at her with a teasing grin. Anything to lure a smile from her.

Thank God. His pack rested in a heap against the back wall. He nearly fell to his knees with relief. "This should hold us off. How about yours?"

"Just some power bars and a juice, but good luck finding it." She roved over the entire den with her light and then paused on his face. "Oh no!"

"What?" He turned a three-sixty, expecting to see another shifter from the way fear flashed in her eyes.

"My father." Aurora froze in place, her eyes wide, the look so raw that for a split second he could see the true Aurora. The one that hurt and felt. Possibly the same emotions he did for her. He hoped.

Adam blinked, shaking his head. Did he hear her right? "Excuse me?"

"His urn, it was in my bag."

Oh. "Where did you leave—"

"Wait, do you see that?"

How could he—she blinded him with her flashlight. "There. In the corner." Aurora pushed past him and fell to her knees by the ice wall.

He moved her to the side, ignoring her protest. "Let me help." Gently, he eased her hands to the side and with a couple of tugs, he risked the vulnerability of the ice foundation to free her duffle. "Damn good eye. Even I missed that."

With a single finger to his shoulder, she paused his choppy movements. Aurora traced along the lines of his den marking. Slowly she outlined the thick claws of the bear that fed into the golden-hued symbol that denoted the den of Wylde. In the wake of her caress, it was like flares of lightning erupted over his skin.

One more tug and her bag slipped free. Blood pounded against his temples and under her delicate touch, his cock grew thicker.

Aurora reached around him and whispered, "Thank you."

"You're welcome." He pushed up and lumbered over to the entrance that led deeper into the den. No use in hiding what his body wanted. Leaning against the wall, he rested his forehead on his arm and inhaled once. Then again.

"I'm sorry, Adam."

He craned his neck around.

"For everything." Aurora stood and wobbled slightly. He reached out a hand, but she held hers up. "I could have come back as soon as I realized my father had no intentions of returning to Claw Ridge, but by then, I don't know." Tears filled her eyes and she clutched her bag as if it were her lifeline. It took all he had not to reach out and pull her to him. To tell her he didn't need an explanation. That having her here now was all that mattered.

He never made a habit of lying.

"When that rogue werebear killed Mother, my father sold off all the assets locally. Or so he told me. I was too naïve. The man didn't make his empire appeasing teenage daughters or by selling off the asset that made him his fortune. By the time I realized that, it was too late." Aurora shivered slightly but he didn't interrupt her. Not yet. "For years I believed we had no ties here, and I let myself believe you would want nothing to do with me even if I did return. Not after what my father did to you and your family."

He'd damn near ruined them. Using the power of his wealth, the patron of the Starr family buried their family business without a second thought. It took years to rebuild and all because he thought shifters were the plague. Bad blood and they had no right to live next to humans much less be a mate to his daughter.

"You tore my heart out when you left, Aurora. There's no coming back from something like that." He lied and it tasted like sand in his mouth, because if asked, there wasn't a thing in this world he wouldn't do for her. "You don't belong in my gritty world. Princesses belong in castles. Not here, especially with a grizzly." He rubbed a hand over the back of his neck and chuckled. "Talk about beauty and the beast." He didn't care what his instinct demanded from him. He couldn't trap her here. She belonged in the lap of luxury. Not wallowing in a den with a werebear. Iron wrapped around his heart, and the walls closed in. "I'm nothing more than an animal. Your father was right—stay away from me." He turned from her.

"Adam Tyler Wylde."

That brought him up short. In his experience, nothing good *ever* came from a woman using all three names to get his attention. As he fought to draw in oxygen he could only stand there, his back to her.

"Feeling sorry for yourself? That's not like you."

"What do you want from me, Aurora?" The gnawing hunger in him grew. If she touched him everything he was trying to do would be for nothing.

Her small, delicate hand rested on his upper arm. Every muscle from his toes to his neck flexed. What the hell was she doing?

"Give me something more, something to let me know you forgive me."

"Like you said, you had no choice."

"What if I did? What if I chose to leave?"

"Then you were a fool for coming back." He broke away. Temperatures were dropping and like hell he could use his heat to keep her warm. That would be the end of them both.

"You have three seconds to tell me what you're afraid of." That brought him around and she stepped back and raised her hand between them as if she wanted to hold him back from getting any closer, yet she was the one closing the distance by getting up in his face.

"You're a fiery mess of contradictions, woman." The way she whipped his name across the short distance separating them made his cock pulse. "Or what, you'll chase me off my mountain? The way I see it, I could have three hours, three days or three weeks. This avalanche could be a foot thick or twenty and whatever you have in that bag won't sustain us beyond a few hours. At best." On the off chance he added, "Unless you have a few Houdini tricks tucked into that suit of yours, we'll be here for a while." Before backing away, he drank in his feel of her irresistible scent. Tingles pricked his skin, burned the length of his back and tightened an iron fist around his balls.

Indifference washed away to reveal hurt, and he caught a glimpse of fear.

Damn. Her vulnerable stance and soft green eyes brought a ferocious need to protect his mate. "Look, Aurora..." Forcing back a shudder from the feel of her soft skin, he gathered her hands and continued in a lower voice. "I'm sorry," he drew out, loving the smallest of contacts. "I didn't mean to scare you and I sure the hell don't want you to think—"

"Forget it. All of it." But her gaze and the way she angled her lips up to his told a whole other story. Despite what she would like him to believe, he heard the note of defeat hidden in her tone. "You must be cold and if you freeze to death, I am NOT lugging your dead ass down this mountain."

There was his spunky girl. "We both know you'd leave me up here to learn my lesson." Relief tipped the scales of his inner turmoil enough to allow a deep breath past the lump in his throat. When she smiled like that, everything seemed to fall into place and honestly, that scared him a bit.

"And you'll have fully earned it for trying to argue with me in your birthday suit." Flustered looked good on her. All red, horny and so confused as to the rush of old feelings. She didn't have to verbalize everything he clearly read in her expressions.

Thankful for the change in conversation, he followed her deeper into the den. "Where are your clothes?" The trickle of fear in her eyes evaporated just as quickly as he'd witnessed its appearance. He looked pointedly at the ice wall. In the shuffle of getting to Aurora in time, his clothes hadn't made it in the tumble. Several hundred pounds of snow probably covered them somewhere between here and the foot of the mountain. "I wish I knew," he mumbled to her retreating back, scratching at the scruffy beard marring his jaw line.

"Tell me about it." Aurora threw a glance at him that could cut the solid ice she wanted to keep erect between them.

"I'm the one who came up here to save someone and here I'm going to be the one freezing," he teased, clenching his fists at his sides to keep from reaching out for her and hauling her into his embrace.

"Should teach you from going all furry and getting into the middle of things." Aurora turned and hurried down the narrow passage that led into the small cutout of a den as if she could sense the danger he posed to her. Not that he would hurt her, but his bear growled with the need to have her pinned beneath him and screaming his name. They could both use the distraction.

"And no one likes a liar. You're no colder than a polar bear in ice water."

He shrugged. That happened to be mostly true. But that didn't help drive home his point.

Heat crawled up his neck as his bear pushed to be freed. With a tight hold over his beast, he clamped down on the instinct to shift. To take and claim.

MINE.

"Aurora," he whispered, closing his eyes. A deep, grumbling roar ruptured inside his brain. His grizzly wasn't taking no for an answer. Too damn bad.

He ground his back molars so damn hard his fucking jaw popped from the strain and traveled down his shoulders until every muscle in his body flexed. Warning flashed across his mind. "Be careful, Aurora. Tease the bear and you won't be safe from me for long." He growled out every last word to make sure she understood his meaning.

She did. The fire in her eyes burned bright and her breath quickened in response.

Good. "Don't say I didn't warn you."

CHAPTER SEVEN

He fisted his hands and closed his eyes. Her scent filled his lungs and caused a rush of pinprick-like sensations to flush over his skin.

If he shifted in this small space...

A whoosh of energy battered his last ditch effort to stay human.

"Ah hell!" Muscles stretched and he fell to his knees. Braced on all fours, his teeth elongated and skin morphed to a full pelt of thick brown fur.

Surprise permeated the air instantly as a sudden gasp hit his ears. "Adam. What the hell!"

He stilled and dropped close to the den floor. With his gaze locked on hers, he inched forward and forced the energy coursing through his body to slow so she wouldn't pick up on the panic eating at him too. Shifting hadn't been in the cards, but resisting her allure proved impossible. As slowly as possible, he tucked his head under her hands. Damn it, he wished they shared the mating bond where he could talk to her in bear form. Let her know he meant no harm. She must be scared.

Maybe if he could get her to relax and see being a werebear wasn't much different from being human, she would accept him.

"Easy Adam, it's only me." With her hands raised Aurora eased away from him and pressed her back against the wall. Hell no, he wasn't having that. As gently as possible, he caught her hand in his mouth. Before he could ease her fear any further she froze, wide-eyed like a bunny caught in a snare.

What the fuck, could he not do anything right?

Smooth move, Adam. Too late to back down now. He released her, dropped his head and pressed his massive head into her thigh until the smooth material of her snowsuit filled his vision. Small, delicate fingers faintly brushed against the back of his head.

It was a start.

Seconds later she spoke to him. "The fur on your belly is softer." He caught her leg with his nose, when she stopped running her fingers through his fur and earned a small laugh in return.

"You gave me a scare, you big brute." All the heat in her words dripped away to reveal a hint of humor. "Next time give a girl warning."

His bear bristled at her words all the same. As his mate, she should never fear him. Hunkered close to the floor, the energy of the shift pulled him through until he stood before her all man. With his arms stretched out, he wrapped her in a hug and buried his nose in her hair. For a brief moment, he returned to the last time they'd stood in this spot. He missed the days he could spend tucked away from the world with only themselves to worry about.

"Adam, there's just too much to say. Too many layers to add yet another one that's even more complicated than the last."

Yet she didn't pull away. Instead, she played with the long hair that brushed his neck.

"Layers were intended to be peeled back, sweetheart. I don't have the energy to deny the need I have for you, Aurora. I can see it in your eyes too."

In a couple of steps he crossed the den and fisted the sides of a folded tarp. Glancing over his shoulder, he caught her admiring the view as he kneeled by the crates. With his acute hearing, he picked up the increase in her heartbeat and a tiny, sexy gasp.

Spreading out the tarp, he made quick work of building a makeshift bed for the blankets and few rugs the locals left behind. "It's not goose down, but it will keep you warm.

"No, it's better. I have a grizzly."

Standing at the edge, he slipped the flashlight from her hands and placed it where the beam hit the ceiling to create a waterspout of light to pour over them. He fisted her hair and pulled her head back gently until he held her mesmerizing gaze. "There's a wild need in me to taste you on my tongue, touch you." He bent to run the tip of his tongue over the shell of her ear as he slid the zipper to her suit down the length of her body. He came to a stop at the juncture of her thighs. "Take you beneath me and..."

"Claim me?" She broke in with a soft voice muffled against his chest. Winding one arm around his neck while holding him off with the other placed over his heart, he felt the tension tighten her delicate body. They were both fighting a losing battle. The only question was when they caved under their fiery attraction, would they get burned?

In two tugs he had her arms free from the confines of her snowsuit only to reveal another sweater with a zipped front. With each new layer he leaned into the brittle barrier of patience separating him from baring his teeth and ripping through every shred of clothing holding him back.

"Adam. Oh God—" She tilted her head back and he wasn't one to decline an invitation. He ran his lips along the juncture of her exposed neck and shoulder. Using his body as a shield from the cold, from the apex of their thighs to her ample breasts, he pressed them together.

"For one night I'm going to bury you with so much passion you'll never want another man to touch you." His fingers tightened. "Before you leave me to go back to your kingdom, I'm going to show you what it's like to have a grizzly shifter as your mate."

Aurora stared up at him, her lips parted. Raspy breaths rushing past her lips. "I'm willing to test that theory, but, Adam," she sucked at her bottom lip, "I never wanted anyone else."

Adam's jaw clenched from the thought of someone else touching her. Enjoying the pleasure of her sweet body. He growled into her ear, pressing between her thighs as he worked her legs apart. She gave under his instruction with a tiny whimper slipping past her lips and an uptick to her heartbeat a mere human would have missed.

As he scraped his teeth along the tender flesh of her neck, Aurora tightened her finger in his hair and pulled him in for a kiss. Searing heat melded them together.

Unable to break away, he slipped his hands between them. With handfuls of soft cotton, he bunched the material and pulled. Instantly her nipples pebbled and teased him through her clothing. Every ounce of blood in his body rushed south.

"You never came for me. Why?" Her arms looped around his neck. There was no escaping telling her the truth with how intently she watched his expression.

He didn't want to do this. Not now. The truth would hurt her. With how innocent she looked up at him, he knew for a fact her father never told her the truth that would break her heart all over again. And it fell to him to do the breaking. Dirty bastard. But holding the truth back would cause a deeper hurt.

"Aurora, never for a second think I didn't try. Your father threatened to disown you if I did."

Shock and uncertainty gazed up at him through her watery eyes. "But all that is in the past," he reassured her.

She blinked, nodding slowly. "I dreamed of you. Every night I thought I could sense you close. But every morning I woke to the same feeling of emptiness." Her expression reflected her quiet words.

"In your dreams, did you stroke your sweet pussy for me? Come for me with my name on your lips?"

"Yes," she whispered close to his ear.

It was all he needed. He hauled her close. Using her several discarded sweaters as a cushion against the cold stone, he pinned her against the wall. Wrapping her legs around his waist, he worked off the last layer, keeping her skin from his touch. With her snowsuit peeled off to hang at her sides, he bent in to taste the delicious fruit his mate offered.

"Adam," Aurora moaned, the sound seeming torn from some deep part of her soul. She gasped the second he wrapped his mouth around the cold tip of her aroused peak. Beneath his touch, her heart raced in time to his own.

Harsh, pent-up growls of his own matched hers. Every muscle in his body clenched as she flexed her hips. The length of his cock nestled between her thighs and the slightest movement nearly brought him to his end.

"Too much. You have too much clothing on."

"Fix it."

"Gladly." He quirked up a half smile. In seconds every stitch of clothing she had made a nice pile on the floor, along with her boots.

Before she could move, protest or rethink her whole situation, he had her in the middle of the blankets. Her parted thighs welcoming him in and several blankets blocking out the cold.

He sensed things were just heating up between the bunny and the bear.

CHAPTER EIGHT

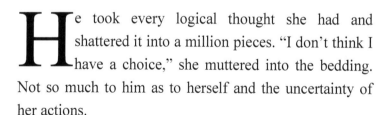

He took every logical thought she had and shattered it into a million pieces. "I don't think I have a choice," she muttered into the bedding. Not so much to him as to herself and the uncertainty of her actions.

The massive amount of heat he put out could melt the snow locking them away from the world.

Somehow, with only a touch and a smile, her own name became a freaking mystery.

God help her. He infuriated her, tempted her controls beyond simply making her want him, and when they were in the same room every decent thought flew out the window and all she could think about was getting her next fix of him. Just like old times.

Losing that much control freaked her out. Considering what he was, what she would become if they mated, that couldn't happen. Her father...

But her father was no longer here to judge her.

"Adam, I want more." She trailed off when the warm confines of his mouth picked up where he'd left off moments earlier when he had her pinned against the wall. With his weight holding her in place and fingers wrapped around her wrists, all she could do was feel. And beg.

"More of what?" She couldn't think. He didn't allow her to think. Only feel. "Please. The other one. More. Yes, more of that."

Battling her unruly desire, Aurora took a deep breath when his lips grazed along the tender flesh of her abdomen until he came to her bellybutton and stilled. Blunt teeth scraped against flesh and metal. A gentle tug to the jewelry caused a rush of liquid to fill her channel. She gasped when a deep rumbling growl quaked the space between her thighs. No vibrator she had felt like that.

"Spread for me, baby." She watched his eyes zero in on her swollen folds where her throbbing clit begged for his attention. He leaned in, the pads of his thumbs spreading her open for him to see all of her.

"I can't. I can't do this." She wanted to scream with all the frustration that boiled inside her.

"What will everyone think of me?"

The walls of her pussy clenched as Adam glided his tongue along the length of her seam. His action spoke so much louder than anything he could say.

Between torturing her and making her freaking crazy, he mumbled, "Does it matter, sweetheart?"

Need to reach between her thighs and relieve the pressure pushed a moan from her lips.

She couldn't decide what she wanted more. Him to eat her until she had nothing left or to have him inside of her, taking her beyond any level she'd ever experienced before.

"Tell me, Aurora, did you let another man touch you, love you. Pleasure your sweet body?"

Love her, no. No one ever affected her like he did. His voice. His intoxicating scent.

"Never," she barely managed.

Back arched, she pressed into the blankets. Fingers tight around the blankets, her toes curled when the roughened flesh of his thumb rubbed a slow tease around her clit. He delved his wicked tongue into her channel as his finger teased her entrance. "Answer me, my beauty.

No lies. Did anyone else have the honor of tasting your honey?"

"Yes. God, don't stop."

"Yes?" He didn't say anything, but the small pause between kissing her inner thighs filled her in on his shock.

"I mean no, no one. Yes. Do more of that," she snapped. She ached, didn't he see that? There was no time for questions. Her hands slipped from the clutch she held on the blankets and sought her diamond hard nipples. With her thumbs and forefingers, she clamped them around the extended buds. Panting, she rocked her hips against his mouth. Another thrust and she'd tip.

Adam rose to his knees, his cock jutted out, thick and long between them. The darkened and engorged head begged her closer, but his devilish grin said he had other plans. Whatever he had in mind, she wanted. For tonight she would savor his taste, his touch and let him close enough to pleasure her once more. She'd have to trust the rock solid barrier around her heart because he was slowly peeling away her layers, and she didn't mean her clothing.

Beneath her fingers his muscles bunched and trembled. A fine sheen of sweat dotted his skin. Kneeling over her, he slowly ran the head of his shaft along her seam.

"Do you like that?"

"Yes."

"Do you want to come for me?"

Instant, all-consuming lust drew a gasp from her lips. Her pussy clenched. Sensations ran the length of her body and doubled up as they settled in her womb.

"Adam. Yes." Everything about her told him that she needed this. Needed him, but she didn't know how to voice what she wanted. She showed him.

Feet on either side of his thick thighs, she reached between her folds and slipped a finger in, then two. With her other hand she stroked his cock from tip to base and reveled in the deep guttural groan she tore from him. Hot liquid spilled from his shaft. She guided him back to her entrance. Lifting her heels a fraction, she dipped her hips and the world narrowed to only that second.

"Fuck, yes," he moaned in a dark, velvety tone. With two fingers he pinched together her sensitive folds to create friction as he entered her. Pressure built as ripples of heat whipped around them. Hard pants tore from her chest. She couldn't handle the need anymore.

"Adam. Adam, please make me come. Take me already."

He pushed in the final inch and seated himself until the tip of his cock brushed against the hidden bundle of nerves tucked within her channel. His girth stretched her tight sheath. It was a pleasure that bordered on pain, tearing through her body with a ferocity she had no hope of controlling.

Or fighting. He thought she lied about taking other men to her bed, but how could she let another man take what belonged to Adam?

He wasn't gentle. She didn't need gentle. Energy sparked between them and settled in the bundle of nerves buried in her core. So hot, so good, and so damn bad for her.

"Just as you reach your peak, I'm going to pull you back until we both can come together and then, after I kiss every inch of skin on your body I'm going to slide you over me and have you take your fill of me. And again, as the sun kisses the horizon, you'll be mine until you have given me every ounce of sweet nectar your body can give. Mark my words, Aurora, after tonight, you'll never want another man to love you."

He came down, his hands on either side of her shoulders. His hair dipped to play at the sides of his face. He drew out and watched her as he slid back in. With each stroke he thrust harder, rocking her whole body with power. An uncontrollable urge to scream built in her chest until she couldn't hold it anymore.

"What... what are you doing to me? Adam!" She shouted his name in a ragged whisper. He leaned back, wrapping her thighs around his waist and lifted her ass off the padded bedding. The angle helped him drive deeper, hit new unexplored depths of her channel.

Shock had her drawing in a deep breath, her eyes going wide with pleasure. Arms tossed above her head, she fell back into his embrace. Rocking forward slightly, he picked up speed. Her breasts ached and she pinched the nipples hard, forcing out a cry. "Oh Aurora, precious, pinch them harder for me." She complied and the effect reached into the very soul. Breathless, she tugged once more and electricity took the direct route straight to her pussy and back in a tantalizing sting. Turning her nipples with her fingers, she rocked with Adam's tempo.

She wanted his mouth on hers, his fingers replacing hers As if he read her mind, he lowered them, hands braced by her head. He moved to cup her ass and angle her up to meet him.

Pleasure reflected back at her through his golden brown eyes. Aglow with the magick of his people, she fought to keep her eyes open but couldn't hold on. Heat flushed through her body. Adam jolted up, holding her to him. Rocked back on his heels, he lifted her up the length of his cock over and over again. "Adam, I can't... can't hold on." Every word slipped out between breaths.

With one hand supporting her back and the other holding her head, he brought her to him. The sweep of his tongue along the seam of her lips had her opening. Warm, and so tender. He took her mouth slow and languid and in total contrast to how he coaxed her juices from her channel with every move he made.

The engorged crest of his thick shaft swelled and stretched her farther. To the point she couldn't feel anything else. The cold, coarse blanket beneath them. Not even her toes. Couldn't focus beyond the pleasures he poured over her senses.

One by one her dreams slowly became a reality. Her memories hadn't failed her, but the sex had never been this... this sensational.

He destroyed her. Built her up and tore her away from the ledge, on the verge of hitting her peak.

Claws extended she dug into his shoulder. With him holding her away from him, the cold swept between them to brush over her nipples. Aurora pressed her hand against the back of his head as his seeking mouth dipped. Molten heat wrapped around her nipple and it was the last thing she needed to push her.

Wild need gripped her core. "Come for me. Give me everything."

Who was she to argue? Spasms rippled through her body and her legs tightened around his waist. His steel arms locked her in place. Quake after quake tightened her pussy around the length of his cock. Fingers tangled in his hair, she tightened her grip and leaned forward into his embrace.

She never wanted another man this way—it was him or nothing.

"Mine. You're mine, Aurora. I can't do this without you."

"You know what I want. Come for me, Adam, Mark me. Claim me."

He cupped both her exposed cheeks and with one final thrust of his hips, ribbons of semen coated her insides. Adam jerked, groaning in surprise as she bent and bit into the flesh of his shoulder with her blunt teeth. Not hard enough to break the skin, but enough to have his cock pulse twice as hard with another shot of his sperm.

"God, Aurora, woman, you break me. So sweet and soft."

"You heal me," she countered.

A faint smile lightened the depth of his eyes, and he laid her out on the blankets and admired her love-marked body before joining her.

As she drifted back to their little world, her lashes opened slowly. His whiskey eyes now glowed amber as he looked down. Something bothered him with the way his handsome face contoured with a deep frown.

"Five years, three months and two days. Do you want the hours too? I know them almost down to the last millisecond." Adam propped himself up on an elbow behind her as his words flowed over her. "Do you know what that does to a grizzly? Being away from his mate that long?"

She angled her body to better see him.

"Have you seen a man so desperate for his soul mate that the life is sucked out of him? Multiply that by a hundred, a thousand and that's the pain I've suffered being away from you."

"I know." She licked at a dusky nipple that had his eyes drift closed for a second.

"Do you?" He groaned and his eyes lit with lust again when he coaxed her gaze to his.

She nodded. And let him look into her eyes to see the truth.

"Your father yanked you out of here so fast..." He trailed off, gathering his thoughts, his thumb tracing small circles around the piercing of her bellybutton. "If it wasn't for my mom gluing the den family together, we would have broken apart."

"All because of me."

He placed a warm palm to her cheek and drew his thigh up the length of hers.

"Because of hatred. Your father judged us all on the action of one and worked hard to ruin us for being different."

"I'm so sorry." Adam lifted his eyes from her lips as she sighed heavily.

"Not your fault, sweetheart."

"What are you going to do now?" She moved her hands down his sides. She didn't want the magic of the moment to fade. If she broke contact she feared reality would rush in and break them apart.

"I don't have a lot of options. All the meetings will have to take place, but after that is done, I'll assume my father's position as CEO and continue on with Starr Gem."

Adam stared off into the darkness beyond their ball of warmth. The haunting expression he wore scared her. "In New York?"

Lightly, she turned him to face her. "That might not be entirely the case. I would have to travel a lot, but Starr Gems can open satellite offices. I mean, I will be the boss," she added with a sly grin that earned her a kiss to the end of her nose.

"I didn't know how to give you this until now." He peeled back the several layers of their cocoon and she immediately felt the Alaskan chill.

Her entire body tensed with a fierce need to have him closer the further he got. She trailed his movements as he crossed the room to gather his satchel. The feeling was a little strange but she liked the adrenaline rush that fed into her blood as he turned back to her. Was it the bond forming like he once explained?

His expression tightened, and the mirth and happiness she saw during their lovemaking swiftly faded. "Promise me something."

"Anything." She canted her head to the side as he produced a white envelope from a front pouch on his pack.

"Promise me you'll do what makes you happy. If that takes you away from me again, so be it. I can live with that. Or, I'll at least try. Whatever your father has to say in this letter, be true to what you want."

Well, hell. Her eyes darted between his and the letter he held. A familiar flourish of black ink spelled out her name.

"Mate me." She didn't want to know what her father had to say right now. What Adam asked of her made everything as clear as the Alaskan sky in the middle of June.

Her words caught him off-guard. That was okay, because it scared her too. But if anything came out of the pain she suffered with her only family, it was to take every day she could with the people she loved. And honestly, she'd never stopped loving Adam.

"Do you know what that means?"

"It means what it should. That I'll be yours and you'll be mine."

"And that your life as a mere human will be changed forever. Can you handle that?"

"What I can't handle is being alone. Not anymore. Not after this." Aurora held up the folded letter. "Not when I have my happiness so close."

Adam rolled her to the side, his delicious weight pinning her in place. "You know you just proposed to me?"

"Blame it on the corporate upbringing, I suppose. Go after what you want kinda thing."

A smile teased his lips. He leaned in and glanced small kisses along her collarbone and over the dip in her shoulder. Between her legs, his shaft grew hard again. The bulbous head already seeking entrance. She dipped and rolled her hips, sinking deeper into the quicksand of desire that threatened to swallow them whole. And she didn't mind.

Strained against her sensitive entrance, Adam paused. "Are you sure?"

"I'm sure whatever the letter says is won't sway me one way or another. I want this. To be honest, I have wanted it since *before* I left. I was just too young to understand. I wanted you the first time you took me right here. The night we lost our virginity together should have been the night we mated. If you'll have me now, we can spend the rest of our lives making up for lost time. Besides, getting furry and having claws isn't such a bad thing."

With a slow glide, he stretched her opening and took everything she offered to him.

CHAPTER NINE

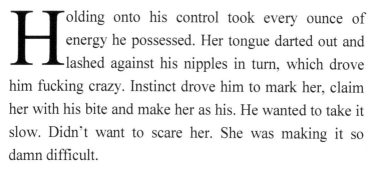

Holding onto his control took every ounce of energy he possessed. Her tongue darted out and lashed against his nipples in turn, which drove him fucking crazy. Instinct drove him to mark her, claim her with his bite and make her as his. He wanted to take it slow. Didn't want to scare her. She was making it so damn difficult.

Perspiration eased down his temple as he fought to rein in his beast. He rose to his knees and pulled her along with him. Swiftly he turned her, spreading her knees wide. Leaned back against him, her back to his front, be brushed the engorged head of his cock along the slippery seam of her pussy. His juices already spilling from her, and it made his shaft grow harder for her. He pulled her long hair to pool over her shoulder and wrapped the strands around his hand, tugging her head to the side, exposing her neck to his bite.

Her lashes lifted and she glanced at him, her gaze satisfied. Kiss-swollen lips parted, he angled her head to his and devoured her mouth. Tasted her with a sweep of his tongue. Her flushed features drove him harder into her core. She licked her lips and cried out.

Holding onto his arm around her waist, she moaned a throaty groan that reached between them. Not releasing the heavy tension tightening his balls was pure torture. Her tight core clutched him with a tight grip.

She pinched her nipples, making her pussy clench around his cock even tighter.

"Fuck, Aurora. You're going to make me come. Not yet. Not fucking yet, woman."

Not yet.

"Harder," she commanded. He delivered.

Her eyes drifted closed as she skimmed her hand over his arm. He shuddered when her kitten claws raked against his shaft as he entered her. His fingers tightened in her hair and he forced himself to slow his pace. His mate had to reach peak with him.

He clamped her closer, raking his teeth along the juncture of her shoulder and neck in time with her nails. God, she made his control slip every second she touched him.

"Fuck it." She had every nerve ending in his body on fire. He couldn't hold on. He growled, lips peeling back to reveal sharp teeth.

She cupped his balls as his teeth broke flesh.

The flesh of her pussy rippled against his shaft. Each shuddering pulse of sensation her orgasm fed her only amplified through him. Electrical tendrils of magick bonded their minds, bodies and souls.

She screamed, her head falling back to rest on his shoulder. There was no going back from this. "Are you okay?" Barely able to think much less speak, he pressed kisses to her temple.

Her delicate body relaxed into his embrace. Gently he laid her out beneath him and scanned her face for any signs of regret. Her eyes drifted open. He couldn't breathe from the beauty that looked back at him.

No longer solid emerald, his mate's eyes now held the mark of an alpha werebear. Shafts of golden rays spiked through her irises to create a priceless jewel.

Reality finally hit in that second. She was his for now, forever.

"Yes, for now and forever, my mate." She touched a hand to the side of her face. "Do my eyes look that different?"

She fell back against the makeshift blankets, parting her slender legs, her folds swollen from the lovemaking. Lightly she stroked a finger down one thigh and then up the other. Swiftly he gripped her hands and stilled her from touching the flesh he owned. If anyone got to play in the aftermath of their lovemaking, it was him. She cocked a brow as if to dare him to do something. "When I get you home, I'll meet that dare."

Her hot little fingers found something else to torture him with as she ran them through his tousled hair. "You failed to mention everything that came with the bite." Aurora ran a finger over the flesh of her shoulder.

"It's something you have to experience to believe," he countered, watching her dazed and mesmerized expression shift to that of surprise and eventually acceptance. Mating a werebear came with a few benefits beyond amazing sex, if you asked him. When an alpha bit his mate, their minds connected. Past memories and feelings melded together to create a unique connection.

"Will you know my every thought?" Her tone didn't give the slightest hint of worry away. Nor did the massive waves of energy forming between their newly minted connection.

He nodded. "And you mine. Does that scare you?" He leaned in and nipped at her bare shoulder. The pink flesh around his bite had already healed over, leaving barely a mark behind. Only enough for another werebear to know she was taken. Speedy recovery was another thing humans didn't have and would take her a little while to grow accustomed to, if her shocked expression was anything to go by.

"I always had you in my head one way or another. This just makes it final." She grabbed one of the blankets and raised up to stare down at him. "Oh my stars! Will I shift? Will it hurt? What color will I be? Will it be the same beautiful sable coloring you have?"

He chuckled, unable to hold back from her excitement. "Unlike my shifter cousins in Sweet Briar Hollow with their witch mates, you'll have your first shift after our first born. The pregnancy will forge our DNA together permanently."

"Children. A family." Her eyes brightened, and he smiled when her fingers splayed over the expanse of her abdomen. Never did he think he would be lucky enough to have his mate come back to him. Now that he could reach out, touch her and love her... everything would change for them both.

"Does that make you happy?" Her answer frightened him more than he realized. If he didn't literally count each heartbeat between his question and her next words, he would say everything in the world ground to a halt.

"Does it make you happy? A little late to ask, but still."

"I can't wait to get you home and make sure our activities produce a little Wylde child." Her laugh warmed him. "Oh, do your cousin's mates change?"

"No, they just share the telepathic connection."

She smiled at that. "Will we meet them?"

"Probably sooner than expected."

He could feel her surprise at his answer before the small skin between her brows pinched together.

"That's a problem for another day. There are a few things a little closer to home we have to deal with first.

"What do you mean?"

"Your admirer from this morning has gotten into some trouble. Trouble he probably can't get out of and resulted in this avalanche. A new resort is moving in on the land your father sold before he passed—"

"Oh no. What kind of problems?"

"The kind that could be problems for the den and Wylde Excursions. They're a shady corporation willing to do anything for a buck. Sadly, so is the ice bear."

"What are you going to do about it?"

"Not sure yet, but it will fall into my father's hands to resolve since he invited him into our den. But let's talk about it later." He reached over her and fetched the folded piece of paper. Right now, they had other things to deal with.

"Sweetheart, when you're ready, you'll have to read this." Aurora's eyes narrowed on the folded envelope he held out to her.

"Let's do it now."

That surprised him. Staring down in confusion, she clarified for him. "If you're with me, I can face anything." He nodded as she continued. "I came here for answers, right?"

He gave a stiff nod. What if what she read in there made her rethink their mating? He bit back a string of expletives and mentally kicked his own ass for suggesting it.

Paper ripped and fear spiked his blood.

Dearest Daughter,

She paused to look up at him, tears already glittering in her eyes. Fuck, she was breaking him.

When I lost your mother, something in me broke. Something snapped and the father I once was morphed into a man afraid of losing something more precious.

You, my child. The thought of losing you drove me to the extremes. Though I am too late, I see this now. At the time, taking you away from the danger was the answer. In actuality, I know I did you more harm than good. I only wished to protect you. One day when you are a mother, my actions will become clearer. Please forgive me this mistake. Forgive me for loving you so much I couldn't breathe at the thought of losing you. Forgive me for taking you away from happiness you deserve. If my final wish has been honored, then this letter finds you in good company. At least let this be one mistake laid to rest with me. Take what makes your heart sing with joy, my child. Everything else will work out.

Love always,

Dad

"Dad. Not father as he preferred after mom died." Tears spilled down her cheeks. Coming to his knees, Adam pulled her to him and held her until the last of her tears dried.

"Thank you." He reveled in the way her soft lips brushed against his chest. That one small connection filled him with hope that he could be the man she needed him to be. Strong.

"Always." Her mind enmeshed with his and the sensations that spiraled through his mate filled him.

"What did yours say?"

He blinked and paused a moment to filter out his thoughts from hers. A sense of anticipation filled his senses and but it came from her. "He said the natural thing a father would. He wished me the same happiness he found with your mother."

"And," she pushed.

"After begging my forgiveness, he asked a favor of me. To take care of the last piece of his heart left on this earth. The real gem of his life." He turned her to face him. "And in some ways he made me a believer again."

"Oh, in what?"

"Happiness. Love."

"Me too."

Off in the distance a whipping sound played at the furthest reaches of his hearing. "Are you ready to go home?"

Lifting her face to his, she leaned in and melded their bodies together as if she couldn't get enough of him. The feeling was mutual.

"Is it possible to stay here forever and a day? Just you and me?"

"I'll do you one better, my princess. How about a forever with me and a family that loves you as much as I do?"

She pinned him with a primitive, possessive look that would scare most men. To him it made his cock pulse with renewed desire.

In the midst of loss the least likely person to bring them together had spent his last breath making sure he had a hand in their fate. Pain had once ripped them apart, but now out of loss, love was found again.

"No matter what tomorrow brings, no matter what the future holds, your princess is here to stay."

Within seconds she had him on his back, his thick cock poised at her entrance. The best kind of trouble he wanted to be balls-deep in.

"I love you," she whispered and sank down until she held all of him with her sheath.

"God, help me, I love you too, Aurora."

"Forever and a day."

"Promise."

THE

END

Want more smokin' hot
bear shifters?

Read on for a sneak peek
at the second book of the
Wylde Den Series

BEAR
HIS BOND

CHAPTER ONE

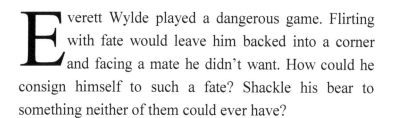

Everett Wylde played a dangerous game. Flirting with fate would leave him backed into a corner and facing a mate he didn't want. How could he consign himself to such a fate? Shackle his bear to something neither of them could ever have?

He took another look at the beauty beneath him and the mark of his den on his shoulder flared with threads of powerful heat.

As the snow melted, the mating season slammed into his hometown of Claw Ridge with a vengeance. Summer, the peak of mating season, was still a month away. By the time fall rolled around again, there was no telling if anyone would be left standing.

Buzzing in his mind grew louder and threatened to drown out everything but the woman tempting the boundaries of his control.

Damn her. Why did she have to be so alluring to his bear? To push him so close to the edge with a simple smile?

Hadn't he promised himself he'd never let anyone close to him?

Whatever had his guts tied into matted knots made it hard to breathe the second her delicate body slid beneath him.

God help him, three days in the backwoods of Alaska with *her* would either leave him drained or dead.

He trailed a single finger over the blackened ink swirls of vines and flowers that decorated the smooth skin from her right thigh all the way up to grace the soft skin of her waist. Sparks shimmered and crackled where his skin met her supple curves. The mark on his right shoulder tingled and spoke to a deeper connection. One he had not felt since the death of his twin.

Damn her.

He flinched and pulled back as if the inked tethers of her tattoo twined around him. Every half hour, like a playlist on repeat in his head, he reminded himself it was nothing more than a fling.

Three more torturous, heavenly days and they parted ways. How many times could he make her peak in seventy-two hours? Would she forget him? Not likely. She returned to her world and he stayed in his. Playboy Everett didn't pine, dammit. But he would make damn sure she did.

Darkness played at the contours of her heart-shaped face pressed into the pillows, and long shadows stretched across the room, barely brushing her golden skin.

The scent of fresh sea air and warm sunshine played with his senses. Some would argue sunshine didn't smell. That was a lie. It smelled like happiness, hope, and a helluva a lot of trouble.

He drew in a deep breath and closed his eyes, working his fingers into the delicate flesh above her hips.

Pepper moaned beneath him and sashayed her hips into his hardened shaft.

The soft, feminine sound reached into his chest and pulled on invisible threads of magick anchoring his heart—good thing too because it lurched in his chest.

A deep growl rumbled up the back of his throat.

Using only the tips of his fingers, Everett grazed a path up the backs of her thighs, over the naked arch of her ass and paused when she shuddered from his touch.

"Beautiful," he rasped. Wisps of her thoughts glanced across his mind. Colorful bursts of light that spoke to the emotions his gentle caresses provoked, but nothing as solid as what mated couples shared. The thin fabric separating him from his beast quivered, and his incisors itched to elongate and mark her as his.

Did she feel the connection forming as well?

She moaned a feminine sigh, and he licked his lips, hungry to eat up her delicious gasps and moans.

He couldn't. No more than he could sink his teeth into her tender flesh and mark her as his forever. He'd already lost too much in one lifetime.

Everett pushed the images aside and ignored the vein in his neck as it pulsed in time with his aching shaft. Gritting down hard, he rode out the wave cutting off his air until he had control over himself.

Every inhalation of her lavender-scented lotion, or whatever she used to get into his head, converted his blood to fire. Oh yeah, his bear loved her scent and roared long and low in his head.

It doesn't mean anything. Any red-blooded man who had this raven-haired beauty beneath him would not be able to resist her sweet moans any more than he could.

It was more than the moans, though. More than how her curves molded into him.

It was her eyes. He'd had handfuls of women, but none of them made him suffer like Pepper Cambridge and her sapphire gaze.

They way she looked at him when she thought he didn't notice tied him in knots for hours. One flick of her gaze his way shot his blood to a boiling point.

Every. Single. Time.

He hated her for it, yet loved her even more. But he stuffed it so damn deep in his mind it made him question his sanity.

Fierce need clawed deep in his gut and he rested his forehead on her delicate shoulder to calm his grizzly.

Pepper was his. For now. It was enough. Had to be. And God, those sweet sighs he lifted from her lips made the impossible seem like his next greatest idea.

He needed to strip it down to what it really was between them.

Mind-blowing sex.

And what is wasn't.

Love.

He'd be safer that way.

Pale Alaskan golden midnight sunlight trickled in from the large window above their heads and fanned across her skin as if Mother Nature wanted to touch the rare beauty of Pepper Cambridge. His favorite time of the year, when the sun refused to sleep. And so did his bear.

Triple panes of glass took up most of the wall instead of a headboard. He preferred the view of his ancestors' land. It also proved a challenge when tying up his willing beauty. The white knit scarf that adorned her hands provided a contrast to her honey-toned skin.

When he'd built the cabin on the back part of Wylde den land, he'd wanted to see the beauty outside. Now he couldn't take his eyes off the treasure it held on this side of the glass.

The way the soft beams kissed the long locks of her hair, stroked along her sinuous bare back and dipped between her parted thighs made his bear rise to the surface, to challenge his decision.

Raw need surged down the length of his shaft. With one hand at the base he slipped the engorged tip through the wet slit of her entrance.

"I love the way you look when you lose all control." He envisioned Heaven as he watched her warm body accept his full length.

She inhaled on a gasp and let out a slow, throaty moan. "You seem to like taking it from me." Sharp nails he loved scraping across his skin now dug into the discarded pillows adorning the head of the bed. Anything within reach fell prey to her tight clutch.

Pulling out, he leaned over her delicate body, stroked the length of her spine with the rough pad of his thumb and took pride in how she arched beneath his touch as his hand slipped between her cheeks to replace his cock.

"Argh, Everett! You're the devil is human flesh." Pepper pushed back into his waiting hand, her words muffled by the pillows propping her up as he worked to prove her right.

"Now, don't be modest. You like my wicked side just a little bit, don't you?" Gently he parted her flared folds and teased her entrance as he showered small kisses along her bare shoulder. The scarlet scarf holding back her sight looked sinful playing in the long strands of her loose hair. If he was the devil, she was his forbidden angel.

Braced on an elbow, he leaned in a little closer to fill his lungs with her scent as he slid first one finger, followed by a second, into her tight entrance, seeking the tight bundle of nerves hidden deep within. In the last few weeks they'd spent together he'd learned what she loved, but more importantly what her body craved. How it responded to a slow, steady teasing. The flush of excitement that swept down her back and blossomed across her cheeks let him know how much he affected her.

What she couldn't know was *how much* she affected him.

Her channel clenched, and he slowed his rhythm. Warm, silky juices coated his fingers. Harsh moans met his ears. He flicked the small nub of nerves between her folds that had her trembling under his touch. He smiled against her shoulder and stroked his fingers back, lightly over her rear entrance between her parted cheeks.

She gasped and turned her head to the side. Those parted lips a shy inch from his. "You don't play fair." Pouted lips and flushed cheeks were quickly becoming his downfall.

"Mmm. Never have. You already know that though."

He brushed his mouth against hers but pulled back before she could turn his teasing taste against him. It was hard enough holding on as it was.

"Is that so? I'm not the one that packed an ungodly amount of scarves." He tossed a glance at the suitcase perched on the end of the dresser. "What could one woman need with all that if not looking for a little foreplay?" he mouthed against the slight dip in her lower back.

Every time they fell between the sheets he courted the danger of losing himself to her.

"When you blush it reminds me of sunsets in the summertime over Starr Point. A mix of sherbet and cherries. Makes me hungry." He nibbled his way up from her lower back.

Not that she could see how beautiful she looked all tied up and at his mercy, but every time she wiggled her ass his heart damn near tumbled out of his chest to lie at her feet, at her mercy. He'd never felt that over a woman before, but there were many things Pepper had been the first with.

"I like scarves, that's all." Her eyes, still dreamy from the sleep he woke her from slowly opened.

"Liar," he countered as he tugged at the knots holding her wrists bound. With his free hand Everett gathered her hands and moved them to the top of the pillows while bringing her legs in closer to her chest. With her plump, rounded backside pressed back against his thighs, she parted for him willingly.

She countered, "So what if I am?"

"Don't move, sweetheart." Her lips quirked up in a half smile. "I could stretch out your..."

"Torture session. Everett!" She groaned with a sigh, wiggling her ass.

He smiled at the desperation in her tone.

"Serves you right for last night." He stroked his fingers deep into the warm slickness of her channel while pressing his thumb against her swollen clit. Everett leaned in and started working her faster. Harder until her core tightened around his fingers.

He slowed, holding back her orgasm.

When she regained her breath Pepper continued if a little shaky, "But you loved me in caramel."

Loved it? One taste of the sweet delicacy of her skin and he could not stop until he had her screaming his name. Several times over. She almost made him cave and he couldn't have that.

Even now his incisors ached to lengthen and tear into flesh. To mark her as his. He'd stepped out five minutes last night after a light dinner to secure the trash and returned to find her laid bare and dessert on her. Literally. Only sheer willpower, not the dainty scarves she'd used to hold him, held him back.

"Now, I get to return the favor." He nipped at her shoulder then lavished the skin with kisses. He tried to convince himself he only wanted a taste of what it would be like to place his mark at the joining of her neck and shoulder.

She skipped the ice cream they'd brought and went straight to drizzling the warm caramel over the peaks of her breast and down the soft planes of her stomach that led him to the real dessert. After she deemed he'd had enough, she took her turn and coated his shaft. When those pouty pink lips of hers parted over his engorged width, he lost all sense of reason.

Unwilling to break contact for a second but desperate for a taste of the sweet confines of her mouth, Everett leaned forward, the girth of his shaft wedged between her folds. He dipped his head for a sample of her kiss swollen lips. He couldn't wait to see them wrapped around him again.

"You said you had a craving for something sweet. I was only trying to help." Despite the blindfold and having her hands tied, she looked the picture of innocence lying before him with her lips pulled between her teeth.

"But you said nothing about what caramel does to you. Wanna talk about dirty tricks. You, my captive, are queen of dirty tricks." And blow jobs. He didn't care to admit it, but every second her tongue whipped against his throbbing cock his blood pressure nearly killed him.

Crimson brushed a wide length up her spine and settled in her cheeks. "I do have a soft spot for the stuff. I should have warned you I like it on everything."

God, he could devour her night and day.

Could this be love? He shook his head and dashed away the joke his senses were playing.

No way. He saw it every day between his older brother and his new mate. It looked nothing like the fling he and Pepper shared. He had to admit, having her at his mercy, beneath him and calling to his bear flared something else to life in the pit of his soul. He dared to let his gaze slide down her arched back to fall on her exposed bottom.

No, this was only lust.

With a hand around her waist, he flipped her over to land in the soft bedding. Having her ass up in the air affected his senses.

Harsh breaths tore from him, and as he stared into her eyes, the surprise he saw gunned his instinct into overdrive. Everything—the wind, the faint birds beyond the windowpane and even the elk grazing a few hundred yards away—hit his heightened senses. As did the faint uptick of Pepper's heartbeat.

She draped her arms around his neck, her tied wrists pressed into the back of his neck. He let loose a chest deep growl and jerked away her blindfold. He bent over, pressing their combined weight into the mattress. "I'm going to fuck you until all you know is my name and the way I make you feel as you reach your end. God, Pepper, stop looking at me like that."

Another whisper of her thoughts brushed his mind and he jerked back, eyes wide. Instead of vague lights and colors this time he saw more in-depth images. Images of him with her with a look on his face that didn't say weekend fling by a longshot. "That's not supposed to happen."

She stared up at him in confusion before her eyes slipped closed. Their thoughts momentarily synced and her pleasure became his. He watched as Pepper realized what was happening.

"What was that?" Pepper tightened her thighs around his waist while her fingers buried into the long lengths of his hair.

He jerked to his knees, taking her with him, and the connection snapped.

"Your eyes. They're gorgeous. What's going on, Everett?" Her voice barely above a whisper but crystal clear to his keen hearing. Hunger and need burned bright in her bright blue eyes. Lava would be colder than the hellfire that flowed through his veins. Heat beyond what a normal man would bear carved a path through him, and his mind shut down for a brief second. One second too many.

Pure instinct filtered his every thought and movement. Blinded by the need to mate, he drove forward and sank his full length into her waiting channel.

Starbursts of lights shattered any remnants of control, and he let the wave of ecstasy carry him through.

Talons cut into his back and the sharp inhale of pleasure from his mate snapped his eyes open.

His heart rate rattled and thumped wildly. Every breathe just as haggard. A sweet ache in his mouth told him his bear was serious about this one.

Hell.

Was this it? It couldn't be. As though anchors moored his eyes closed, he fought back the encroaching takeover of his body and slowly regained enough control to withstand sinking his teeth into her flesh and bonding her to him.

That could never happen. Not if he wanted to live beyond loving her.

He pulled his gaze away from her. "Just feel, sweetheart. Let me carry you away. Trust me." Though he didn't recommend it. Tying her to him meant she'd lose in the long run. Offering her all of him meant more than he could sign on for.

As he spoke, his lips moved against hers. He captured her moaned acceptance as he delved into the sweet confines of her delicious mouth.

With an arm around her waist, he held her close and groaned when her fingers tightened in his hair as he took their kiss deeper. He slowly relented control and gave over to her curious exploring. Anything to have her focus shifted from what just happened. He didn't have answers to give. But he did know how to answer what her body asked from him.

She met his thrusts as he drove into her long and slow.

Damn the Draeonians and their meddlesome ways. As first otherworldlies, they discovered the power hidden within the ley lines that crisscrossed the planet and bound the strongest of spirits to the human race fierce enough to wield their energy. Dragons, witches, shifters, fae—they all derived from the same forces of magick. In order to keep a balance within the energy gifted by the supernatural forces of their planet the Draeonians also destined werebears to mate with humans. But no one ever said finding their true mate would be out of his control and damn near instant. That was the part he didn't like. Instinct didn't need to drive him into the arms of a woman. That part was his choice, not some invisible force he had no control over. And no desire for.

He pulled out and peered down his chest to see the crest of his cock slip from her channel, her swollen folds parted around him.

Spread wide, he ran the tip of his cock along her seam and groaned when the scent of her arousal hit him full force. It was all he could do not to slam into and ride her hard, all finesse shoved aside for another time.

He reached beneath her and cupped her ass, angling her up, and in one thrust settled his full length in her tight sheath. Muscles trembled around him and nails bit into shoulders.

He broke their kiss and reached behind him to free her hands.

Even though they didn't share a full connection, he could feel the hum of her thoughts as they reached out, searching for the connection he knew she didn't understand. As if his bear worked on forging a bond despite his efforts to stay disconnected.

He rose to his knees, and emerald eyes warmed a point on his chest and begged him to look her way. He could feel what she wanted without the words. His breath quickened, and his heart damn near tumbled out of place. But he kept his gaze glued to his cock as Pepper took his full length.

He eased back and thrust home.

"Like what?"

He worked his dry throat while she took all of him into her.

"What?" He brought his head up. How could this woman keep any thought straight at a time like this? What did he miss?

Pepper waited patiently, watching, hopeful and waiting. "Don't look at you how? Like I want you to promise you'll erase all my memories of sex with anyone else?" She reached between their bodies and wrapped her delicate fingers around his shaft. Sweet heavens. He groaned and nearly lost himself when he pushed back in. Her channel clenched around him, replacing the tight grip of her hand. She nearly had his eyes rolling out of his head.

"Seems fair *if* you don't stop until I'm all you can feel beneath you. Until you can't think anymore, no?" she continued, unaware of the internal war tearing him apart. Otherwise, he was pretty sure she'd be trying to give him CPR.

Instead, she gathered handfuls of cotton as he tightened his fingers around her sun-kissed thighs and buried himself deeper.

Tingles of magick coursed through him, and the mark on his arm flared with invisible current.

Fuck.

Balanced on his knees, he pushed forward as he pulled her in closer, her legs wrapped around his waist. His efforts returned with a deep moan and the sight of her beautiful breasts thrust in the air sent a surge of blood south to engorge his cock further.

He'd meant to take things slow. Enjoy a nice plane ride, show her the sights while she performed her job as a wildlife veterinarian. The second her pink lips wrapped around his shaft at three thousand feet over the national reserve, slow was no longer an option, and his meticulously laid out plan to distance himself took a steep nosedive.

"God, woman, you're so fucking tight and wet. Fuck... so wet."

He hauled her into his arms to rest on his spread thighs. She sank deeper onto his shaft, and he marveled at how the dusky tips of her breasts beaded under the soft, warming sunlight.

Anchoring her thighs tight around his, and with his hands firmly on around her waist, he lifted, driving in as she tightened her hold with her thighs. Everett spoke her name on a whisper. Just like yesterday she loved taking control as much as she loved giving it.

He rewarded her wicked, daring look with a flicker of a smile. "If you make me come too fast, I'll fuck you again and this time I won't untie you until I've had my fill." It would kill him, steal every ounce of control he harbored but anything to see the look of pure, unabashed ecstasy in those deep green eyes.

Desperate, he ground his knees into the bed and fought the urge to come until every breath they took came out ragged and torn and they were both coated in a fine sheen of sweat. Claws raked over his shoulders and back. He drove into her harder, earning him a few more love marks. His balls drew tight against his body.

Gripping his hands, Pepper's head fell back and the loud scream of release came just in time. Hot ribbons of his sperm released into the confines of the condom as her core quaked around his shaft, extending his orgasm.

After long seconds, with her hands pressed into his shoulders, Pepper let her head fall back. Hand to God, the sun caught her raven hair in a way that made him swear he had an angel in his arms.

They fell back against the mound of pillows, and he pulled her closer still. She began that maddening play she did with her fingers along his tattoo when she wanted his attention. Mesmerizing, but the more she touched the mark of his den, of his ancestors and the mark he shared with his lost twin, the more he wanted her. The more he couldn't have her.

"Does it count if we come together or do you still want to punish me?"

Everett took a long breath. His devilish angel would be the death of him.

(End of sneak peek)

To continue reading make sure to pick up the second Wylde Den release, Bear His Bond.
Available in eBook and print.

Want more smokin' hot shifters
and misadventures with magick?

Read on for a sneak peek
at the first book that kicked off the
bestselling MoonHex Series

HEXING THE ALPHA

CHAPTER ONE

"This better work or else we'll be finding a new place to call home come next month, Cinder."

Honor gathered a pinch of crushed lavender and sprinkled in the last of the ingredients needed for her love potion. A puff of purple smoke twined high before diving back into the concoction that would— fingers crossed— work this time and play cupid for a very lonely woman. "Fourth time's the charm. I hope." Honor tucked a stray strand of hair behind her ear and let out a deep sigh.

She'd promised her client a spell that would convince her boyfriend to take the last plunge toward marriage. Success would net her a cool two grand—enough to save her bar and the attached apartment.

Getting the spell to work was proving to be more difficult than she'd anticipated. All three previous batches had fizzled out along with her patients.

If she didn't get this to work soon it was bye-bye to the only security she had and hello cold streets of Sweet Briar Hollow. Panic sent a cold shudder down her spine and she wiggled her toes nestled inside her favorite warm wool socks. She still had time. Twenty-four hours to be exact. Her gaze fell to her hands as she splayed her fingers out to call forth her magick, searching for a little calm in her own personal hellish storm.

Encased in the magick-tinged wave of heat that flooded her body came a rush of power laced with memories of the last time she felt so much energy in her palms. Sweet, delicious, mind-blowing, pure masculine strength in the form of the sinfully sexy alpha pressed up against every inch of her body. Goddess, she so did not need this right now.

An unbeckoned smile spread across her lips. "Stop that, Honor." She flexed her fingers and forced herself to focus. Had it only been three nights ago that he'd almost taken her? Her core still vibrated with pent-up need for him.

No, what she needed was to forget him. Forget the way his lips ignited a fire in her belly. Forget the way her body had molded into his embrace. The way his gaze, luminous with a red tinge she didn't understand, pulled her into his world. Body and soul.

But more importantly, forget how he'd left her wet and wanting, spread open for him on her bar top with a growled, "Sorry, pack business."

Yeah, forgetting one Jake Monroe, alpha shifter, wasn't likely. She took a calming breath and counted out her heart beats to steady her thoughts.

The Hollow in the winter was like living in Antarctica, and served as a damn cold bucket of water to her runaway thoughts. In fact, she was pretty sure the below freezing temperatures of her small Maine town rivaled anywhere else on the planet come January and no amount of lusting after Jake would change that for her.

Honor tossed a look at the clock hanging behind her couch. Almost time to open the bar. She rolled her shoulders and called forth the five elements that fueled her powers, the call of fire her strongest. Heated energy crackled and popped in the small dining room, fusing the air with enough juice to power up ten love potions.

She needed this to work. Maybe the spell just needed a jump-start. "Worth a shot anyway," she murmured softly.

A long drawn out growl from the chair where Cinder lounged watching the whole fiasco punctuated her thoughts. His black and orange patched fur was fluffed and bushy with static. "Hey, not long now and don't give me that judgy look, buddy. We need the money and this," she wagged a finger at the bubbling cast iron cauldron on her dining room table, "is the only way I know to get the fast cash we need and to keep kitty nip on the shopping list."

Her feline familiar blinked once as a human would shrug his shoulders.

Sassy pussy. Whatever.

She needed to get on with this before one –or all—of her three sisters dropped in and found her mixing the forbidden concoction. Not that they would turn her into the Council, but it would definitely put them all in a pickle if ever questioned or placed under a truth spell. Nasty things truth spells, and very commonly used on witches with rebellious pasts.

She was well-acquainted with the rules governing her kind and right now she was breaking about five of them, which would get her kicked out or worse, stripped of her powers by the Elders. Not cool. But she didn't see any other choice.

It wasn't as if the Council issued loans. So here she was. Solving her own problems if only *slightly* against her world's law.

Before starting, she had flicked the deadbolt in place and stuffed a towel beneath the doors, windows, and every other crack she found in the old apartment to help hide the odor. One of her sisters was bound to stop in for a drink and her efforts would do little in holding them at bay once they smelled the sweet nectar of rose and lavender. If they did show up before she finished... well, she'd rather not think about how many different ways this could go sideways tonight.

Honor dipped the tip of her pinky into the swirling mass of fuchsia liquid laced with variant shades of midnight purple and popped it into her mouth.

Much like her favorite Pop Rocks candy, it tingled along her tongue and down her throat as she swallowed the single teardrop worth.

Mmm. She sucked the single digit between her lips and sighed.

Dazzling white heat burst to life, singeing her insides to finally detonate in the depths of her core with a powerful need she'd never felt before. She swayed in place and let her eyes slip shut. Just as quickly the all-consuming sensations calmed, leaving behind a blanket of warmth to settle over her entire body like a lover had left her thoroughly sated.

Would finding release with Jake be that wild and untamed?

Honor shook her thoughts clear of the sexy alpha.

"Thank the goddess this actually has a chance!" She pumped a fist in the air and received a swish of a tail from her plump familiar. "Cheer up, Cinder. I think we're almost there. Just a few final touches."

Honor scrolled a finger over the spell she'd penned especially for this task until she came to the last part needed to bind the spell to find true love.

True love. She'd be happy if she could get one devilish sexy shifter to look her way one more time. No love particularly required, but in some ridiculous corner of her mind a roguish shifter to call her own did have a nice ring to it.

If anything his sapphire eyes and midnight black hair spelled wild lust-filled nights. Her feminine parts quivered just thinking about the broody male that had spent the better part of the last month holding down the back corner table opposite her bar top.

Damn the goddesses. She knew to the bottom of her soul, they'd had her in mind when they cooked up his wolfish charms and good looks. Her body thrummed every time she felt him track her movements as she tended her customers. His eyes had a way of glowing with an ethereal light every time she glanced his direction. Raw heat is what she saw in their depths and it made her naughty side crave a little dirty romance.

She couldn't quite wrap her mind around the why, but when their gazes connected nothing else mattered. For that split second between serving a drink or some other task at hand, everything dropped away and she only saw him, the force of his gaze like the smack of her love potion to her senses and her thoughts of total possession. She just didn't understand it. Maybe she didn't need to. Maybe it was leftover feelings from the night they almost shared.

She didn't fit under the ranks of saints. She'd had wild nights of hot sex before, but Jake made her feel different. As if what he wanted would be beyond mind-blowing. If only she knew what had sent him hoofing it out of her bar and away from her when they were so close to finally taking their attraction to the next level.

Did he not feel the same way? If he did, the wolf had a damn good way of hiding it.

She paused and looked down at her handiwork.

The potion. It was playing with her emotions and churning up the hottest passions buried in her soul.

She let out a deep sigh. "Here comes the fun part. Time to nudge destiny a bit."

She closed her eyes and dashed thoughts of Jake to the back of her mind where they damn well better stay locked away. With her attention refocused on fusing the potion with her binding powers, Honor interlaced her fingers to form a barrier over the opening of her cauldron and started.

With this spell I declare
A single drink to claim a heart so fair
A perfect match bring forth this night
With a heart pure in light and a wish
for love so true and right
For the good of all and with free will I
cast this spell to do my will
As I enchant this potion with my words
So let it be done and that it harms no one
So mote it be

Flashes of purple and magick-laced fire brought her eyes open. A single flame spiraled up from the liquid, then absorbed back into the confines of the pot to shimmer with her infused power.

Done.

"Now if only by the goddesses it works…"

From the shelf above her refrigerator, Honor snagged a silver container she normally reserved for the homemade liquor the *other* locals preferred. Shifters burned through what she had on tap so she cooked up her own brew that kept her doors open. Barely. Her illegal love hooch would keep her in the black for now, but for how long? She couldn't sell enough of the regular booze to the locals and stay afloat. Her only hope now was her ability to attract more shifters with her special brew of Moon Lust.

She measured three servings of the love potion into the container, then sealed the bottle. She placed the canister on the table by the front door and turned to the mirror to straighten out her hair from the messy bun she sported, planning her next move... delivery and payment.

(End of sneak peek)

To continue reading make sure to pick up the first MoonHex release, Hexing the Alpha! Available in eBook, print coming soon.

A Note From Talina

Dear Reader,

Thank you for reading *Bear His Mark!*

Aurora has a few more secrets to reveal and Adam's adventures have only begun now that he's mated. You'll be seeing more of them as we get to know all seven Wylde siblings in the stories to come.

Next up, when a Wylde bad boy falls, he falls hard and Everett is about to learn how wrong he is about love and mating in Bear His Bond. Truth be told, the Wylde brothers aren't the only ones that fall hard. I'm nursing a huge crush on the Wylde men and I hope you love them as much as I do.

I hope you enjoyed reading the first chapter of Everett Wylde's story, Bear His Bond, and the first chapter of Hexing the Alpha, the first book in the MoonHex magickal series that shares the same world as the Wylde Den series.

To make sure you don't miss a release or the upcoming Draegonstone series you can sign up to my newsletter on my website at www.talinaperkins.com.

Xoxo

Talina

Also by Talina Perkins

WYLDE DEN SERIES
Bear His Mark
Bear His Bond
Bear Their Secret
Snowbound with Her Christmas Bear

Other Available Series

MOONHEX SERIES
Hexing the Alpha
Jinxing the Alphas
Bewitching the Alpha
Enchanting the Alpha
Charming the Alphas

SEXY SIESTA SERIES
(Military Romance)
His By Sunrise
Tequila Sunset
Sunrise for Three

ABOUT THE AUTHOR

Talina is a bestselling author of military and paranormal romance. Her stories are deeply emotional and touch the heart while heating up the romance between the sheets. She writes about sexy alpha shifters, hunky military men that make falling with them irresistible and kick-ass heroines that love a good challenge!

Born and raised in Mayberry USA, this small town country girl spread her wings at the young age of fourteen and moved to Mexico where she's lived for the past eighteen years. Now, Talina currently resides in sunny Puerto Vallarta with her four children and is married to a U.S. Recon Marine—her very own smokin' hot hero.

Talina also writes sweet romance as Roma Frost Hart. You can find out more about her forthcoming releases on her website at www.romafrosthart.com.

18063436R00083

Printed in Poland
by Amazon Fulfillment
Poland Sp. z o.o., Wrocław